THICKER THAN WATER

ALSO PUBLISHED BY PEEKASH PRESS

*So Many Islands: Stories from the Caribbean,
Mediterranean, Indian and Pacific Oceans*

New Worlds, Old Ways: Speculative Tales from the Caribbean

Coming up Hot: Eight New Poets from the Caribbean

Pepperpot: Best New Stories from the Caribbean

THICKER THAN WATER

New writing from the Caribbean

—

Edited by Funso Aiyejina

PEEKASH
PRESS

Published by Peekash Press
Copyright © Bocas Lit Fest 2018, 2021
Copyright for individual texts rests with the authors
All rights reserved

Paperback ISBN: 978-1-63614-021-6
Hardcover ISBN: 978-1-63614-022-3
Library of Congress Control Number: 2021940032

Peekash Press
14 Alcazar Street, St Clair
Port of Spain
Trinidad and Tobago
www.peekashpress.com

Akashic Books
Brooklyn, New York
Twitter: @AkashicBooks
Facebook: AkashicBooks
info@akashicbooks.com
www.akashicbooks.com

Commonwealth
Foundation

the
bocas
Lit Fes
MORE THAN A LITERARY FESTIVAL

CONTENTS

ABOUT THE HOLLICK ARVON

CARIBBEAN WRITERS PRIZE

The Hollick Arvon Caribbean Writers Prize, which ran from 2013 to 2015, was an award which allowed an emerging Caribbean writer living and working in the Caribbean to devote time to advancing or finishing a literary work, with support from an established writer as mentor. Sponsored by the Hollick Family Charitable Trust, the prize was jointly administered by the Bocas Lit Fest and the creative writing organisation Arvon.

The prize awarded writers in three literary genres over consecutive years, announced at the annual NGC Bocas Lit Fest. The winners were Barbara Jenkins (Trinidad and Tobago, fiction, 2013); Diana McCaulay (Jamaica, non-fiction, 2014), and Danielle Boodoo-Fortuné (Trinidad and Tobago, poetry, 2015).

EDITOR'S NOTE

Funso Aiyejina

Thicker Than Water celebrates some of the major new voices in Anglophone Caribbean literature. It is a multi-genre anthology of writing by writers shortlisted for the Hollick Arvon Prize for Caribbean Writers, which was awarded between 2013 and 2015. Contestants had to be Caribbean by birth or citizenship, and had to be living and working in the region. The aim of the prize was to discover and nurture new talent. In addition to the cash prize, winners were given the privilege of working with agents, editors, and workshop facilitators to prepare their works for publication. Each year, the international panel of judges, made up of academics, editors, agents, and lovers of literature, got the opportunity to read and judge works from emerging Caribbean writers and to facilitate their exposure to the world.

What is evident in the works brought together in this book is the commitment to new ways of seeing by the writers. These are writers who encourage us to see beyond the lapping coastal waves, the white and off-white beach sand, the startling sunrise and sunset, and the riotous street colours pervasive in popular images of the Caribbean, to the intangibles that truly define the region. Their subject matter is seldom the grand historical events of previous writings from the region. Rather, they meditate on the need to confront family secrets; the absurdity of religion in the hands of men and women lacking moral moorings; relationships (some personal, some political) waiting to be named and embraced or denounced; and invisible fault lines. Their gaze is on the termites silently eating away at the heart of the wood. As poets and fiction and creative non-fiction writers, their quarrels with their enabling communities are fuelled by a desire to speak their truths as eloquently as possible. There is a subversive self-critical wink running through many of the pieces, and, from the ratio of male to female writers (three men to sixteen women), this book is underscored by the ascendancy of the female gaze in contemporary Caribbean literature.

At the level of both theme and style, many of the works in this anthology talk to, and/or play tag with, each other. Hence the mixed-genre arrangement of its contents. But genre-purists who would prefer to have intra-genre conversations can easily do a genre-by-genre reading.

Neither the prize nor this book would have been possible without the generosity of the Hollick Family Charitable Trust and the support of the Arvon Foundation. Also, because of the small size of the Bocas Lit Fest organisation, almost all of our projects require input from most members of the team. In the first year of the competition, Patrice Mathews performed the role of prize administrator. This job was taken over by Anna Lucie-Smith in the second and third years, and she also functioned as the coordinating administrator for this book. Both Nicholas Laughlin and Marina Salandy-Brown were active participants in the various stages of prize administration and book production. I would like to thank all of them and the other members of the Bocas team for making this book and our other projects possible. Thanks, too, to our judges who were called upon to read and assess a large number of entries within a very short period — pro-bono! In my capacity as the chief judge for the Hollick Arvon Caribbean Writers Prize, as well as the editor of this celebratory anthology, I would like to thank Edward Baugh, Ruth Borthwick, Fred D'Aguiar, Jennifer Hewson, Caroline Hollick, Clive Hollick, Sue Hollick, and Godfrey Smith for their participation in the judging process — who also, by so doing, accepted our invitation to occupy front-row seats to witness the emergence of these writers.

Thicker Than Water confirms that the Caribbean is blessed with quietly penetrating, effortlessly urbane, and socially committed prose writers; environmentally passionate and historically anchored creative non-fiction writers; and thematically courageous and stylistically daring poets who manipulate language to create poetry that is daring, engaging, fluent, and confident. These are writers who are emotionally complex and critically engaged. They are the heirs to a multi-storied and multifaceted Caribbean literary tradition that is as multi-chromatic and multi-layered as its complicated history. These writers boldly engage with a Caribbean that is not constrained by its clichéd images of sea, sun, and sand. They are products of their history but they are not hog-tied by it. Here are writers who see what many do not see and dare to speak what many fear to think.

Five Rivers, Trinidad and Tobago

THREE POEMS

Nicolette Bethel

THE REVIVALIST POCKETS LILY'S RING (1916)

They pray like prophet in the oil-lamp light:
this Annie, smooth and brown, beside a child
who shell skin gleam and shine to spite
and spit her betterment about in oiled
rebuke. A silver glint below that white
slim neck pull Portia's eye. Without a smile,
the child quick-finger it, and pray. Skin-bright,
this Lily tilt her head, unreconciled
to the darkness around.

She grasp that ring too tight.
The thin chain snap
and link and ring roll wild
into the dark.
The smoky lantern light
swallow them all.

Portia, revivalist, smile.
Return by day, she say.
you find it then—
and stoop
and palm the ring
and smile again.

The Suicide Sobers Lily's Son (1950)

One thick night some daughter come to the window
of the room he don't share no more
and call for him. They don't know
how his head soar high and light, a hot air balloon
floating safe above pain, over death,
lifting memory away to the anaesthetic moon.

They just say:

> Mark come quick.
>> Daddy gone upstairs
>> and nobody could wake him—

They don't say:

>> Rust spreading on the ceiling
>>> Mummy weeping in her bedroom
>>>> Daddy leave us mumbling
>>> goodbye
>>> I love you
>>>> hell

•

Now Lily don't sleep. She use to sleep
some long-ago time when she have a husband
and a second son. So when she hear the whisper
and the bedspring and the footfall
she rise from her bed and follow.

She watch her lost lost son
climb up the next-door staircase.
She watch her Mark turn soldier at the top,
see him kick the lock, split the jamb, bust on in.
Lily watch him reel back out before she turn away.

•

So she don't see him straighten up, his head no longer air,
his nerves all buzz to life by half-forgotten smell
of blood, of waste, of human death.

And she don't see Mark close the door or block the stair,
tell the daughters, hold the wife. She don't see him
soldier his step to bring police. She don't see
him help them take the suicide away in the cold light

of an empty dawn.

She don't see him march on home

or take her bucket to the cistern,

draw clear water,

take her scrub-brush

clean

Mister Fountain lifeblood

from the next-door neighbour

upstairs floor.

THE LODGER BREAKS LILY'S RULES (1974)

To go from Sunday speedboats, water-skis
and weekend trips to distant cays, Saturday lolling in bikinis
sipping forbidden Martinis
with strong-jawed men in swimming trunks, stealing kisses
with little thanks on half-deserted beaches
matching roving hands with wishes
to this?
A narrow bed in a narrow room
and the narrow mind of this woman whose home
is choked with Bibles, lectures, strictures, shame?
And why?
Who decided I should stay
so out of the way,
in this crook-wood, lean-to, coldwater house
where one can't lose
even the sheerest pair of pantyhose?
What punishment is this?

Each bright morning Lily tiptoe past the double bedroom door.
The wooden floor
creak beneath her feet
and still the shift-shift of the sheet

beyond them door. Lily does stop, does still

her breath, does gather all her patience for this girl. Nicole

fifteen and still at school, with one last year

to balance out her future.

Lily rooms done empty

and money hard to come by,

and banker cheque from Singapore are welcome for a time.

The girl been left behind. So Lily share her home.

And lodgers pay far more than bill;

they fill

the empty space of these ghost-fed

wall awhisper with the dead.

But this girl?

Last night we went out dancing. What a night! My head is all awhirl

with nightclubs, sweet hands, liquory tongues,

the pressure of some hard-limbed man's hot thighs, and songs

are ringing in my temples. The window's closed again.

It took the tottery laughter of two men,

a makeshift jimmy, slipping hands,

a tingly knee

upon the windowsill, a tickle on the secretest part of me,

an olive-gin goodbye

to get me in.

Our giggles brought me joy again.

What sin

is it to laugh? My father left with his new wife,

and Asia's no good place to start a life.

It'll take more than this old bat's belief

to stop me.

Why?

Outside the door

Lily sigh a prayer

and move away.

SOPHIA'S NEW SHOES

Lelawatee Manoo-Rahming

The sun had not yet come up, but the dawn light was bright enough for Anu to make her way to the river. She wanted to bathe and return home before the sun peeped over the hill that shadowed the pool, before the rest of the village stirred. Anu knew how easily rumours started about who was crazy or who was obeah woman. She did not wish to be seen walking about in the dim morning hours. She did not want to add to the rumours.

After undressing to her underwear, Anu lowered her overheating body into the dark, green pool and sighed as the water immediately chilled her body. As she floated, her mind slipped back to another morning, forty years earlier, and she wondered why she was so afraid. Why couldn't she dive in after Sophia? Anu asked herself. Why was she scared of this same green pool, in this same river, whose coolness she now craved?

Although she wished she could stay in the river all day, Anu emerged from the water, and, without drying off, pulled on her soft cotton dress. She knew that her body would heat up again and her clothes would be half-dried before she arrived home even though it only took ten minutes to walk home. No one ever told her about the hot flashes. No one ever warned her that before she knew it, she would be fifty years old and her body would feel as if it were shutting down and every so often, without notice, her body temperature would spike and she would imagine her body to be like a piece of coal glowing red just before it burst into flames. Even though each occurrence lasted only a few minutes, she would long to immerse herself in the coolness of the river. That was the main reason she came back. The pull of the river was stronger than her fear. It was that, and Sophia's shoes. Forty years later, Anu was still looking for them.

The road from the river to Anu's house was a dirt track, same as it was when she was a child. Her house was over seventy years old. Built by Anu's grandfather, her nana, it was the first concrete house in the village of Never Dirty. Before getting married, he built it for his bride, his pretty dulahin, as he called her. Anu's grandmother, her nani, used to tell her stories from before she was born. Her nana was a farmer, growing tomatoes, cabbage and pigeon peas on his small plot, which he sold in the San Juan market. He had insisted on using all his savings to build the house. He wanted something more than the tapia house he had grown up in, or the wooden houses that everyone else in Never Dirty village had lived in. He was a proud man like that, Anu's nani used to say.

This house was where Anu's mother was born and grew up and where Anu herself was born. But, according to her nani, when Anu was two years old, her mother had to find work in order to take care of herself and Anu. The money her nana and nani were making selling in the market was not enough to feed all four of them. Anu's mother found work as a live-in maid with a family in Valsayn, a rich neighbourhood, that she had to take two buses to get to, and left Anu in the care of her nani and nana.

By the time Anu arrived home from the river, the day was

already too bright. Even at six in the morning, the daylight was sharp and burned her skin. She sat in the gallery to rest and soon a young woman, smartly dressed in a red and blue work uniform, walked into view.

"Good morning, Elise," Anu greeted her warmly. But Elise quickened her step and walked past without responding. Anu could not blame her. All Elise would have been told was that the Francois and Maraj families did not speak to each other, not after what Anu did to Sophia.

"Is alright, Elise, I go keep the greeting for when you need it," Anu said without any malice. Elise was the spitting image of Sophia Francois, the image that had been haunting Anu for forty years.

Anu rose and went into the darkness of the house, glad for the refuge. The darkness reminded her of the little room, with one small window, in which she and her mother had lived when Anu was sent away to her mother in Valsayn. It was the maid's room at the back of the large house of her employers, a white family called De Verteuil. The De Verteuils were kind enough to let Anu stay with her mother. They had insisted that Anu should go to school. But it was the end of July, with a whole month of summer vacation still left. In that month, Anu's mother was able to enroll her in the Spring Village Hindu Primary School, which was close enough to the house in Valsayn for Anu to walk to school.

During that first month when she went to live with her mother, Anu spent most of her days in her mother's dim room while her mother was busy with her work. The only furniture in the room was a bed against one wall, a small table with a chair against the opposite wall, and a wardrobe. Above the table, a mirror and a picture of Goddess Lakshmi hung on the wall.

Anu spent hours sitting in that chair looking at the picture of Goddess Lakshmi, whose face reminded her of Sophia. It was not that Sophia resembled Goddess Lakshmi, it was just that the curl and colour of Goddess Lakshmi's lips made Anu think of Sophia's glistening pink lips, which looked like sweet, ripe guava flesh. Sophia was creole with curly black hair and light-brown skin. Like Anu, Sophia, her brother and sister did not know their father. They, along with their mother, lived with their mother's parents further up the road from Anu's house, around the bend in the road, in the house where Elise, Sophia's niece, now lived alone. Sophia's mother had a day job so she did not have to leave them and go away. Sophia's mother did not work on weekends so she stayed home and made sure that her children stayed home too.

One Sunday afternoon, as Anu played alone under a large chennet tree across from her grandparents' house, she heard the neighbours talking.

"She does keep them home when she home but that don't prevent them three children from gallivanting all over the place on their own after school, instead of studying their books," one neighbour said.

"Is because they grandparents can't control them," another neighbour added.

"The little girl grandparents can't control she either. They does let she spend too much time in that river, if you ask me," said a third neighbour.

"All of them children need they father and them to put some licks on they behind. To straighten them out. Stop them from running wild all over the place. That is what you does get these days when them woman and them have children without father. I tell you, something bad bound to happen, you mark my words," warned a fourth neighbour.

At the time, Anu did not understand what the neighbours meant or who they were talking about. Years later, when she remembered those snippets of conversation, the voices sounded like whispers, as if the leaves on the tree were talking among themselves, and Anu did not know if the voices came from up the hill, down by the river, or across the valley. But she figured out one thing: they were whispering about her and Sophia.

But how could those neighbours have guessed how much Anu loved to feel the coolness of the gently flowing river water caressing her body? How could they have possibly known that when she emerged from the water, the goosebumps on her body made her shake herself open to the sun, like a flower opening at dawn? And that was how Anu and Sophia became best friends. They were two little girls, growing up together, as free to ramble as the morning glory vine, who loved bathing in the river. Could those neighbours have foreseen Sophia's new shoes, too? Did anyone know then that the image of that pair of shoes would stay with Anu for the rest of her life and that she would fondle that memory as if it were a real pair of shoes, because it was the only thing of Sophia's that she could call her own?

After Anu was sent away from Never Dirty, she never went to another river. The De Verteuils only went to the beach, mostly Maracas Bay. Although Anu looked forward to the outing, bathing in sea water was not the same as bathing in river water. She always felt hot and sticky if she could not immediately rinse off with fresh water. But she liked those beach limes because the only Indian food the De Verteuils enjoyed was dhalpuree roti with curry goat or chicken, which they insisted on having for their beach picnic, and which Anu relished because it reminded her of meals with her grandparents back in Never Dirty.

At eleven years old, when Anu wrote her Common Entrance Examination, one year after she enrolled in Spring Village Hindu Primary School, she failed. Mrs. De Verteuil said it was no wonder, for who could pass any exam after going through the kind of trauma the child went through? Two years later, Anu received her school-leaving certificate and her school days ended. Anu then spent her days helping her mother.

One day, an Indian family, the Singhs, who lived two streets away from the De Verteuils, and who had heard that Anu could make good dhalpuree roti, asked her mother if Anu could work with them. Her mother said yes, but Anu could see her eyes blinking quick, quick, and knew her mother was worried.

"You know I don't want to send you away from me?" Anu's mother asked. "You know I only want to keep you safe, right?"

Anu nodded.

"But you can't stay here too much longer. You need to find a job. With the Singhs, you would have a place to work and stay. You go be close enough so I could see you often, and keep an eye on you. Even though you fifteen already, you still too young. You is still my piti popo."

Once, Anu had a boyfriend. The family who lived opposite the Singhs had a young gardener working for them, and often, as she swept the driveway or did some other work in the yard, Anu would glimpse the young man across the street. Sometimes he would look at her and smile. Eventually the two of them started talking and soon he was bringing her little gifts of whatever fruit was in season: plums, or guavas, or cherries, or julie mangoes, her favourite.

His name was Raja. One day he asked if Anu would go with him to the Drive-In theatre to see the Indian film that was showing that weekend. Anu and her mother frequently went to the Drive-In to watch films because they could easily walk there. Although Anu was already eighteen and older than her mother was when she gave birth to her, Anu still asked her mother and Mrs. Singh if it was okay for her to go to the theatre with Raja. They both said yes but Anu searched her mother's face and sure enough the sign was there: her mother was blinking quickly. Her mother was not sure she was doing the right thing by letting her go to the theatre alone with Raja, Anu thought. But neither her mother nor Mrs. Singh had said, no, and Anu was excited to go to the theatre with Raja, to be like other young people. Plus, she liked Raja, who she thought was as handsome as any Indian star boy.

At the theatre, Raja offered Anu his hand and guided her up the stairs in the dim light, to the balcony where all the young people gathered to watch the film. He bought popcorn and sweet drinks for both of them. Anu's heartbeat quickened each time she reached for some popcorn and felt Raja's hand brush against hers. She was not sure about this new feeling: a little scary but tingling, almost as if she was entering cool, dark river water, in the early morning, except, instead of her body getting cooler, it was getting warmer. Anu hardly paid attention to the story and the lyrics of the film because she found it difficult to follow the English subtitles on the screen, with all those unfamiliar feelings racing through her body. Still, she was caught off guard when Raja brought his head close to hers and whispered, "I could kiss you?"

Anu froze. She did not know how to answer his question. He must have taken her silence to mean yes, because his lips were suddenly on hers. She shut her eyes in fear. But instead of darkness, Sophia's face appeared. Sophia's face, as large and animated as the faces on the theatre screen. Sophia was laughing loudly, her upturned face wet with river water and Anu was holding her hands tightly. No, Anu was not holding Sophia's hands, she was holding her shoes, one in each hand. No, Anu was not holding her shoes, she and Sophia were together holding her shoes, as if playing tug-of-war with them. The shoes were the only things between them.

A sour taste rose in Anu's throat. She jumped up and ran. She ran down the stairs, out the theatre, past the guard at the exit, and all the way home to her little room.

The next day, when Raja came to work, he refused to look at Anu. She was so confused and scared, she did not know what to do or say. So she did nothing. Nothing at all, almost as if she had been paralyzed by Sophia's image. Not long afterwards, Raja stopped coming to work and Anu later learnt he had found a new job. That was the end of her boyfriend episode. She never had any other boy show any interest in her.

So there she was, fifty years old and alone, in a little village behind God's back, living in a crumbling house, and haunted by the face and shoes of her childhood friend, Sophia. Now, each morning, as Anu cooled her body in the river, she relived her childhood days with Sophia: all the bird whistles, tweets and coos; the hummingbirds, bright like jewels, and the rainbowed battimamzelles flitting above her head; the gurgling of the water flowing over the bronze-coloured rocks; the different green shades of the trees and plants; the little red crepe coq flowers and even the white of the Maraval lily that grew along the river banks, all of which had not changed in forty years. It was as if time had stood still in the river. It was as if Sophia still lived in the river.

Anu remembered that morning when she and Sophia went to the river. Even though they were both the same age, Sophia was always the leader. She was the one who tried everything first, even eating unfamiliar flowers, or seeds, or fruits, and coerced Anu into imitating her. She would walk along the slippery, moss-covered rocks, balancing with her arms, and every so often she would lose her balance and Anu would be scared that Sophia would fall and hit her head on one of those rocks. But, somehow, Sophia was always able to make sure she fell into the water away from any large rocks and she would laugh, squawking like a parrot, when she hit the water. If Anu was hesitant or refused to follow her, she teased her and called her a scaredy-cat. But Sophia always avoided the deep, dark, green pool; until that last morning.

Even before they got to the river, Anu could tell that Sophia was more feisty than usual. She talked nonstop without giving Anu a chance to say anything, and she skipped along the road from side to side almost as if she were dancing to some wild music in her head.

Anu had to run to keep up with her. As soon as she reached the river, Sophia waded into the pool and disappeared into the dark water.

"Sophia! Sophia, don't do that!" Anu shouted, staring at the spot where Sophia had entered the pool. "Sophia, come out, I can't see you," Anu cried. "Sophia!" Anu shouted even louder.

And then Anu heard her laughing on the other side of the pool, where the river was once again shallow.

"Anu, you is one big cry baby!" Sophia sang.

"And you is one wajang girl! You so wild," Anu snapped with anger. "Why you carrying on so today? What happen to you?"

"Nothing ent happen to me, is what I getting today," Sophia smiled.

"What you talking bout?"

"I getting new shoes today. My mama say when she come home she go bring shoes for me."

"Why she giving you new shoes? Is not your birthday yet."

"She say she see a nice pair of black shoes with little red bows that go make me look pretty." Sophia reentered the pool and made her way back to Anu.

"But you pretty already."

"I go look prettier, then," Sophia smiled and splashed water on Anu. "You still vex with me, Anu?" she asked quietly, reaching out for Anu's hands.

Anu let Sophia take her hands because she could not stay mad with her for long.

"Come in the pool with me, it nice," she cajoled.

"No, I frighten."

"What you fraid? Is nothing in the pool. I done swim right through it."

"It too deep and dark."

"I will hold you."

"And then you will let me go when we reach in the middle. I know you, Sophia."

"That's your business then," Sophia replied and waded away from her to a large rock near the edge of the pool.

"What you go do with your new shoes?" Anu could not get the shoes out of her mind. She wished she were getting pretty new shoes too.

"I go wear my new shoes and I go skip and dance like this," Sophia said as she stood on the rock on one leg with the other bent at the knee, and twirled. Sophia twirled and twirled and twirled.

"Stop, Sophia, you making me dizzy."

"No!" Sophia shouted and jumped into the pool.

"Stop it, Sophia! Come out of the pool now," Anu cried. But Sophia did not emerge from the pool. Anu kept her eyes on the other bank to see where she would emerge from the pool, but Sophia did not come up.

"Sophiaaaa!" This time Anu knew something was wrong but her fear of the pool kept her from diving in. "Sophia, where you? Sophia, come out now!" Anu shouted, but there was no sign of Sophia.

Anu could think to do only one thing. Run. She ran up the road straight to Sophia's grandparents' house. She never could recall what she said to them but she remembered running back towards the river. She remembered that some of the young men from the village were running with her. Anu remembered the young men pulling Sophia from the pool. She remembered them trying to resuscitate her on the river bank. And she remembered her nani and nana holding her, almost dragging her home, as she screamed, "Sophia, no, no, no, Sophiaaaa!"

Anu's nani and nana put her to bed because they did not know how else to console her. Anu cried and cried and cried. Then she fell asleep. The next thing she knew, her nani was waking her.

"The police want to talk with you," her nani said softly.

"Why?"

In her grogginess, Anu had forgotten about Sophia.

"They want to ask you about what happen this morning."

Like all the other children, Anu was scared of the police. The only time they ever saw policemen was when there was a fight in the village and Anu would run and hide because her nana and nani used to threaten to let the police come for her when she was being naughty.

"Just tell them what happen," her nani said calmly but Anu had never seen her bite her bottom lip so hard.

In one breath, Anu told the policemen all that she remembered. "You push Sophia?" one of them asked after she stopped talking.

"NO!"

"You sure?"

"Sure, sure, sure! Cross my heart and hope to die!"

After the policemen left, Anu's nani gave her some fever grass tea sweetened with condensed milk, and a piece of sada roti with tomato choka. She drank the tea but left the roti and choka. Then she told her nani she wanted to go back to sleep. Her nani let her go to sleep even though it was the middle of the day, and Anu had long stopped napping during the day. When she woke up, it was dark but there were voices coming from the gallery.

"Mr. Maraj, I want to talk with Anu."

"Sophia Mother, I really sorry about Sophia. Anything you want me to do?" Anu's nana asked. Even though her nana was older than Sophia's mother, he showed respect by referring to her using her eldest child's name, an Indian custom he knew since he was a child.

"I want to talk with Anu."

"She sleeping, Sophia Mother," Mr. Maraj replied.

"I want she to tell me what happen."

"I done tell you what she tell the police. I really sorry." His voice broke.

"Well... I don't ... I don't want to see she... round my children no more," Sophia's mother stuttered in between sobs.

"The police say she didn't do nothing wrong, it was a accident," Mr. Maraj explained.

"The police? What police know? All I know is my daughter dead and your granddaughter is the last person to see she alive. What I must do? Oh God, what I must doooo?" Sophia's mother wailed.

When she quieted down, Sophia's mother slowly said to Anu's nana, "I don't want to see she at the funeral. As a matter of fact, I don't want to see you and your wife neither."

Then Anu heard a rustling, as if someone were taking something out of a paper bag.

"You see these shoes, Mr. Maraj, I buy these shoes for Sophia today. This morning I tell she I was bringing shoes for she this evening. What I suppose to do with them now, eh, Mr. Maraj? What I suppose to do with them now?"

"You could put them on she for the funeral."

"Mr. Maraj, you can't tell me what to do with my child shoes! As a matter of fact, I don't want them no more. If Sophia can't wear them, they will rot in the bush!" Sophia's mother must have flung them into the bush by the pommerac tree because Anu heard a crashing sound in that direction.

After Sophia's mother left, Anu came out of her room, and, without letting her nana and nani see her, she took a flambeau and went searching for Sophia's shoes. But she could not find them. She gave up and decided to search again the next morning.

The next day, however, when Anu awoke, she saw that her nani had packed all her clothes in a little grip. As soon as she finished breakfast, her nani bathed and dressed Anu, who protested that she could do that herself. Then her nani and nana took Anu to her mother at the De Verteuils' house in Valsayn. Anu never had a chance to say goodbye to Sophia, never had a chance to find Sophia's shoes.

In the six months since her return to Never Dirty, each morning as she walked to the river, bathed in the pool and walked back home, Anu relived that morning when Sophia drowned. And she thought of all the things that Sophia never saw because she never had a chance to leave Never Dirty. She wished Sophia could have seen the powder blue of the sky and the deep blue of the sea at Maracas Bay from high up on the mountain road. Or swim with her through the rolling waves in the wide bay surrounded by the tall mountains, sometimes dotted with orange when the immortelle trees bloomed. Inevitably, the tears streamed down her cheeks.

One morning, after arriving home, Anu decided to sit and rest on the back steps, away from the glare of the sun and away from the road. Sitting there, she had a full view of the pommerac tree in the yard. The ground was covered with purple-pink flowers from the tree. It was then Anu saw that the yam vine had dried up, golden brown against the magenta blossoms. She found a cutlass and started digging gently, scraping the soil, looking for the full yam. Soon she spotted the silvery brown of the yam skin, and, using the flat, dull side of the cutlass, she carefully cleared around the yam until she was able to lift it out of the ground. She sat back on her haunches and examined her produce. Suddenly, Anu gasped. In the soil, caked in one of the folds of the yam, was something reddish. On looking closer, Anu realized it was the rotted remains of a little bow. She started digging with her bare hands and soon found the remains of the other red bow and the two little black shoes.

Anu knelt beside the hole, which to her mind was now a little grave, with the pieces of the shoes clasped to her breast, rocking back and forth and crying. She cried until her tears dried up. Then she rested the remains of Sophia's shoes in the hole, refilled it with earth and covered the spot with pommerac flowers.

"Goodbye, Sophia." Finally Anu was able to speak those words aloud. She breathed a deep sigh, and resolved to go to Elise that evening. She would tell Elise the whole story. She would tell her about her aunt, the well-loved, little Sophia.

FOUR POEMS

Danielle Boodoo-Fortuné

Doe

The Hunter Remembers the Doe

You see, her eyes spoke
but I didn't listen.
It happened like this:
The dogs leapt,
seized her by the throat.

I pulled the trigger;
turned her face into

the damp earth
so I wouldn't see her eyes
while I did my work.

But once I drew the blade
against her side, I knew.

It was still warm, breathing
deep inside the half-moon
of her open belly.
"Leave it", someone said,
But I couldn't. I feared
the darkness would swallow me,
that the sighing trees
would remember my face.
It blinked twice beneath
its caul of wet silk, looked
right into my blindness
with eyes that spoke
the same language
as its mother's.

The Hunter's Wife Remembers the Fawn

When he brought me the fawn
that Sunday evening,
its weight in my arms
felt somehow like prayer.

Its eyes were like yours,
difficult, hungry,
heavy with the memory
of its mother's ruined body.

But the truth is,
it was you who broke my heart
that night, you with your small hands
made for holding on too long.
You didn't even make a sound
when, startled by its aloneness,
the fawn thrashed and split
its skull on the kitchen floor.

The Hunter's Only Daughter Hears the Fawn Song

There is music in the forest,
a word I heard the bush tell.

It is a single sound,
a song for the barefoot
and the aching of heart.

They say once you hear it,
you shed your old tongue
and learn to speak
in the soft whoop
of the lonely.

They say once you hear it,
you lay yourself down
beneath the trees,

and the fawn is the one
walking home
in your skin.

HOWLER

Even if you never wake
inside this flute of light
this whip of green, whistling
the first god's riverine
alleluia

there still must be
the need to howl.

You feel it on mornings
in the taxi's damp chest.
It starts beneath your feet,
humming thread of need
rising up your spine.

Behind the glass now, you are
a creature dull-eyed and
crookedly tamed.

Here is no land
for wild beasts

let the silver cross
round your neck and
the blade in your waistband
bear witness.

so what is there to do
with the surging flood
of this day

but to turn your throat into
a gourd that must hold it?

Even you must know this:
everything that breathes
will howl.

UNLOVED

Ira Mathur

I

Trinidad in the 1990s — Victoria's nursing home

In the long-shadowed, finely brocaded dust of late afternoon, against the charcoal-rimmed outline of the sea, I head to Victoria's nursing home to see Burrimummy, my grandmother.

She was once known as Shahnur Jehan Begum. And then Begum Pasha. Those days are over. Now, she is "Baig".

To get to the nursing home on Mucurapo Road in St James, I pass the Catholic church on Long Circular Road, weave through the familiar streets of St James — Delhi, Calcutta, and Mooniram, a patchwork of indentured labourers' memories from India. I drive past the St James temple, translucent white, lit lovingly by the keepers, a powerful symbol of the Hinduism that destroyed Burrimummy's life; past the mosque in the compound of the Jamaat Al Muslimeen, home to 114 men charged with murder, treason, and an attempted coup.

Victoria's Senior Residence is a two-storey building for the aged, painted in a hardly visible beige, bearing a plaque that it was "inaugurated" by the late Archbishop Anthony Pantin in 1990. It is inhabited by some two dozen people of both sexes, and all colours, in varying degrees of decay.

This is Burrimummy's second visit to Trinidad and Tobago, tiny twin islands in the Caribbean, seven miles from Venezuela, thousands of miles from India.

This time, she arrives half dead. Her blood sugar is so unstable she nearly dies. There is no one in India to look after her. Her heart is failing. Her kidneys are failing. She needs to be near a doctor round the clock. She has wounds that are not healing. She needs nurses. As soon as she's stabilised, I will take her home.

Burrimummy's quarters, the large room she shares with five other "residents," which must at one time have served as a drawing and dining room to a family, is clinically clean and smells like a hospital ward. The bed sheets and the nighties and pyjamas worn by the residents are stiff with detergent. A sickly floral air-freshener mingles with sweetish stewed chicken and macaroni over a foundation of human excrement, sweat, and urine; pine disinfectant rises from the terrazzo floors.

The ground floor has been knocked into a large open-plan room laid out to maximise space with beds and cupboards with the residents' names on them, and, for those like Burrimummy who need it, commodes.

Outside, a searing tropical noonday light, its shadows stunted, blanches the walls. The contrasting dark indoors turns the old people into stick insects, until the eye gradually picks up details — mottled faces, veined hands, papery skin with the imprint of bones. The patients, sometimes grandiosely referred to as "residents," are sitting, staring, standing, and lying about, a blur of dark stick shapes. One is wandering off in a confused way to sit on other people's beds, abuses the nurse who guides him back. Another is inert, watching TV with unseeing eyes.

Burrimumy is doubled over in her corner bed into her usual C shape, legs half falling off the bed. She never lies down flat. A defiant energy in her keeps her legs hanging to one side, sometimes one foot touching the floor, her inert body on the bed — as if her stay is transient, as if she is ready to get up and walk out at any time.

I sit on her bed and rub her back to let her know I am there, paying penance until she decides to acknowledge me. A dim light transforms the home into the set of a stage.

She awakens, slowly, like a drugged woman, but takes everything in at once. With me, she doesn't play the games she does with my sister Fairy — like call me "nurse" and pretend not to recognise me. She needs a bath badly. Her thin white hair is stuck to her forehead, wet with perspiration. I know she is cleaned up after using the commode by a brusque unseeing nurse, who wipes her charges with toilet paper, not caring that drops of urine or smears of faeces may have stuck to their skin for hours, or days until the next bath. She smells.

I catch the nurse's eye.

"Can you please wash her hair"?

"There is no more shampoo."

"I've been asking them for THREE days to wash my hair. They say they DON'T have shampoo and I know Fairy has brought lots."

"Shampoo done. Every day she wants her hair washed and I wash it."

"She doesn't, you know. She doesn't."

I look from one to the other, waiting for one to trip the other.

"Please, bathe her; please, wash her hair."

"I go see if I have time."

She walks off. I stand, not knowing what to do. Burrimummy speaks in Urdu.

"That woman," she says, pointing to the nurse, "is always pushing and shoving me while cleaning me, changing the sheets."

"She pushes you, Burrimummy?"

"Yes."

"Have you had dinner?"

I look at the untouched plate by the side of her bed. Creamed spinach, macaroni pie, and a piece of sugar-browned chicken.

"No, I'll have bread n' butter."

I run to the kitchen, to the nurse sitting down with a cup of Ovaltine, her swollen feet on another chair.

"I'm so sorry to bother you. Can she have some bread and butter?"

The nurse looks at me as if I am mad.

"Please."

"I heard you the first time."

"She will get sores if she's not clean."

"I don't thief."

"I'm so sorry. Please. Look, she doesn't know what she's saying. I believe you. I know you look after her as best as you can. I will bring more shampoo."

I take out a hundred dollars.

"This is for the shampoo for when it runs out."

We both know shampoo costs twenty dollars.

"I will bathe her and wash her hair tomorrow."

I go back to Burrimummy. I watch the clock impatiently while I am around her. I can't wait to leave this room filled with the wrung out, flaccid rinds of human bodies.

One by one, the nurse is drawing curtains around the beds in the rooms, to get them ready for the night

"What did you bring?"

I display my offerings, the treats of our childhood that look inadequate and shabby here. The purple grapes, slightly withered; the yoghurt, out of a plastic tin; the honeydew melon, cut in half; a faded muddied lemon; and a bottle of coconut water.

She goes very quiet. It's thinking quiet. I know something's coming. Then she commands attention — the way she has all her life, with a simple "You know . . ."

I wait.

I start feeding her the yoghurt.

"You eat."

"No, I've eaten, Burri."

"Mumma died forty years ago."

"No, Burri. Twenty-four years ago."

"There was something wrong with her brain."

Pause.

"Mother talked such rot. She always talked rot. And she gave Father hell. Mumma only drank buffalo milk. It's much creamier than cows' milk. She was fat and lazy and sat all day reading the papers. She was so English she should have married a Britisher."

The nurse brings a sandwich with squares of processed cheese between two slices of white bread.

Burrimummy starts chewing with her gums, knees in the air like old times.

"You know, darling," her belly shakes, the way it used to in anticipation of laughter. "When I was getting married I got fantastic presents. Mumma kept a tab on everything, getting our secretary Mastaan saab to write it down, and pack it carefully away in various suitcases. The only thing that was missing by the time we set out on our train journey out of Hyderabad to Bombay was a solid gold alarm clock encrusted with emeralds given by the Maharani of Jodhpur. We all hunted and hunted and nobody could find that clock. You wouldn't believe how we found it."

She waits.

"Please tell me, belovedest," I say, overcome with happiness. She's back, I think. She's back.

"We had almost the entire train to ourselves. I was asleep with my sister Nazmeen and our cousins Ayesha and Mahbanoo. The ayahs were sleeping in the corridor. Suddenly, in the middle of the night, we were awoken by a whistling noise. We thought we had arrived, but when we looked outside it was pitch black and the train's wheels were thundering beneath us at such a pace. Ayesha got up and hurried down the corridor and the noise followed her. Mother started to shout and soon all of us, including the ayahs went behind her. When we finally got to the end of the train, she sat down and covered her ears. Mumma reached into Ayesha's blouse like a master detective, pulled out the alarm clock from under the folds of her sari. Ayesha pinched it. Mumma would have liked to thrash Ayesha, but that would be like admitting to the world there was a thief in our family."

I am laughing. Burrimummy's body shakes with silent laughter. I lean over the bed and clutch her. She clutches my arm. I think it's because she's still laughing but she's leaning on me to make her way to her commode. Once on it, she slumps. There is a terrible smell.

I call for the nurse to clean her up, trying hard not to show my disgust.

"I want water on me," she says.

I wait outside the bathroom as the nurse washes her on a chair.

She deftly makes the journey back to her bed, where the sheet has exposed some of the mattress. Hunched over till her torso is almost parallel to the ground, half monkey, half moko jumbie — the Carnival character on giant stilts. She uses alternate hands, resting solidly on a table, to reach across to the wall, resting on the wall to reach to a bedpost. Before I can fix the sheet, she collapses; allows her full weight to drop. Her walk, instead of emphasising her frailty demonstrates her steely skill at surviving.

II

The Nawab of Mysore and Burrimummy, India, 1970s

It is 1974. We hadn't been to Cunningham Road for a long time. It is a Bangalori day: cool, heady with crushed fallen fruit, decaying juices mingling with damp earth and petrol sputtering from Burrimummy's little black Deccan Herald. Burrimummy drives into the dusty circular driveway of Mysore House on Cunningham Road, past a sprawling lawn with a rose garden, a swing under the spreading jamun tree, benches and a marble fountain of a woman pouring water from an urn on her right shoulder. She parks under the tall pillars of the garage wound with ivy and wood roses, patchy with yellow peeling paint. We are visiting the Nawab of Mysore, Abdul Azeem Khan, the elder of my grandmother's two brothers.

Burrimummy's youngest sister, Nazmeen Pasha, lives with Nawab Abdul Azeem Khan. Her younger brother, Abdul Walid Khan, lives on the other side of town with their mother, the dowager Begum of Mysore, who is now ill, in a nursing home. The two brothers don't speak. They have quarrelled over property.

Trailing behind Burrimummy, I can see Simran, my great-uncle's wife, and Nazmeen Pasha, my great-aunt, draped on the godums on the velvet-covered thakath, a large square sofa good to sprawl on, even take a nap on.

Simran, Burrimummy's sister-in-law, waiflike in a chiffon sari. She reclines like the women in mogul paintings.

The whitewashed pillars, the wisteria, the piano that can be glimpsed indoors, are just a background to her delicate beauty. She's never noticed me. She has stopped laughing. She is looking out at her garden, like someone bored from watching the fountains. She looks mournful, an expression Burrimummy says is natural if you're beautiful. Now delicately sipping her nimbu pani made with limes from trees in the garden. Simran ignores us without trying.

Nazmeen Pasha, hook-nosed, in a blue dressing gown, is spitting tobacco. She is a dark, smaller version of Burrimummy, with that same voice that's powerful and musical at once, a similar belly-juggling laugh, the same orange paan mouth, perpetually chewing, stained with tobacco. This resemblance is strange. Burrimummy's Nilgiri cream skin is the opposite of Nazmeen's caramel skin; Burrimummy's face doesn't have Nazmeen's hooked nose and thin lips. Nazmeen never married. After her father died, she was passed on like a responsibility to her brother, the present Nawab of Mysore.

I feel protected by Burrimummy's powers as she strides up the verandah stairs in her starched cream cotton sari and pearls.

The girlish ayah on her haunches, her two oily, skinny arms trailing, polishing bits of the marble floor of the verandah, nearly topples over in an effort to make her salaam extra low.

The greying ayah serving Simran hurriedly transfers the tray to her left hand to accommodate the right-hand salaam, spilling juice on the tray.

Nasmeen aunty's voice, eerily like Burrimummy's, directed at the old ayah, rings like bells.

"Don't wipe the tray with your filthy sari, oh child of a pig. Bring fresh limejuice for the Begum. No, don't take back that glass. Give it to Begum. Clean that up. God, you people are uncouth."

The ayah rocking baby Yaseen, the Nawab's youngest child, to sleep on the swing moves her protective palm from the baby to raise it to her face. The third ayah massaging Nazmeen's plump thigh retrieves one hand to salaam to Burrimummy.

"Say salaam to Mummy Darling, and to Safu Mummy," Burrimummy says. I bow my head and put my right hand on my head by way of greeting. No grownup sees me. Burrimummy clutches Fairy's hand, shields her as if she is under potential attack.

Fairy leans into Burrimumy, sucks her thumb. She is as sacred as the cows the Hindus worship on the road.

I hear my great-uncle the Nawab of Mysore's voice before I see him.

"Shahnur, have you had a poke lately?" He is reclining on an easy chair with a glass of scotch in his hand, and bares his full paan-stained rust-coloured lips and teeth.

"May you be damned in hell," she says, but she is smiling.

Burrai Mamujaan, big uncle, is Burrimummy's younger brother. He is six feet six inches tall, and sounds like he has a gong inside him with each word he utters.

Now the Nawab roars with laughter, orange paan smeared around his full lips. I hover, anxious about Burrimummy's exchange with her brother.

The Nawab, who spends his days in important work, investing in stocks, whisky in hand, ignores Fairy, spots me and sings loudly, "Well hello, Dolly."

I squirm behind Burrimummy.

"Well, well, Zia's daughter, aren't you going to say salaam to the Nawab of Mysore?"

"Salaam," I whisper, standing behind Burrimummy, who pushes me forward. Burrimummy and Burrai Mamujaan say in a brother-sister chorus, "Say it properly. Adab sai. With manners."

"Salaam walaikum, Burrai Mamujaan."

"Walaikum salaam, Dolly," says the Nawab of Mysore. Orange paan and tobacco spit land on my white socks.

Nazmeen nods sternly at me as if in warning, for what I don't know. She reluctantly wishes Burrimummy, only half rising, flicking her wrist in greeting.

The exquisitely mannered Simran gets up and does a cursory salaam that reflects how little she thinks of Burrimummy, then sinks back into the fat sausage-like pillows on the square velvet-lined thakath that Burrimummy said were brought to India by Mogul emperors.

The Nawab of Mysore is standing over the women. A chair is pulled up for Burrimummy. She sits as straight-backed as if she were at a piano. I place myself of the edge of the thakath.

Fresh orders arrive. Burrimummy is sipping a froth of soda water and ice. I get a Coca-Cola. The ayahs are still moving about.

Nazmeen is talking through her laughter, her pan spit going everywhere.

"Our aunt Basheer hated her daughter-in-law Lulu because she was a Parsee. Lulu loathed cats. Early one morning, Basheer sent huge trunks full of cats and got the servants to fling them into her son Khusro Jung's garden. When Lulu opened the door to go for her morning walk there were hundreds of them running everywhere into the house. She screamed for hours, even after the servants cleared them out. She was absolutely furious and never spoke to Basheer again."

The Nawab gets up.

"Where are you going, Baba?"

"To have a bloody piss, Naimoo. I can't do pishaab sitting down, can I?" Nazmeen says, matter-of-factly, "Walid and Azeem both did pishaab in the ayah's mouth when she was snoring away."

I find that funny. I laugh and laugh thinly, without sound. No one hears me.

Burrai Mamujaan asks, "How is Mumma?"

They are speaking of my great-grandmother, after whom Fairy is named, dying in a nursing home in Bangalore.

The room goes quiet.

Burrimummy says, "Walid says he can't pay for her nursing home bills."

Nazmeen cuts in, "Before father died, he TOLD Walid not to rely on the privy purse."

Burrimummy agrees with her younger sister, "Puppa remained loyal to both India and the British, and in the end they kicked him in the teeth."

Nazmeen says, "At the party for the Nehrus at Colonel Tandon's house, Palkhivala, the lawyer who drew up the act that stopped the payments to all the rulers during the Raj, said, 'I'm so sorry what I've done to you, princess.' I asked Palkhivala if his 'sorry' could bring back my father's broken heart and my back to him."

The Nawab says, "Because Mrs Great Gandhi took away the privy purse, even the Nizam of Hyderabad came to nothing — lives in Australia on a farm. Remember Safu, that flawless emerald peacock in Falaknuma Palace that he had made for the Viceroy and Lady Willingdon? We went there for dinner. The British stole everything and whatever was left, that bloody Indira Gandhi has taken."

Burrimummy says, "I can't pay Mumma's nursing home bills. What am I to do? I am a widow living alone with these children of Zia's. Serves Mumma right. She brought this on herself. Dying in a nursing home with unpaid bills. Why the hell is she penniless? Because she gave all her jewellery to a stranger in Hyderabad, stitched gold coins in her petticoats, and took them away under Puppa's nose to some dead doctor's family. But Baba, the bills have to be paid."

Her brother reaches for his inhaler.

"I can't do anything, Shahnur jaan, my life. My stocks and shares are doing terribly. The house is falling apart. This is no way for a Nawab to live, with only fourteen servants. I've had to sell so much already. I've got a family to look after."

He heaves, pants.

Simran says, "Azeem darling, here is your inhaler."

He sniffs with each nostril, takes another sip of his whisky, looks exhausted.

The baby wakes up with a yell. Simran looks pained. Nazmeen shouts, "Damn it, haven't you given baby a bath. She must be crying because she's filthy. Go on, take her in."

As the ayah disappears into the drawing room, Nazmeen screams after her, "Make sure the water isn't too hot." She shouts again, "And wash all that russum and idli smells off your hand." She turns to Burrimummy and says, "These South Indians are impossible."

"Naimoo, you must never wear burgundy. It makes you look like an ayah." It's a sly reminder of Nazmeen's dark skin.

A golden darkness descends in the garden, a buzzing flying insect shoots in front of me, as if there is no time to waste.

Holding his glass out to the butler, who comes running up to refill it, the Nawab says looking at Nazmeen, "She thinks wearing a thin dressing gown will get her a poke, or a husband."

He laughs uproariously at his own joke and Burrimummy joins in. Simran smirks delicately.

From the verandah I can see the tiger skin in the drawing room and a gloomy cluttered room. What was a poke? Something a man did to a woman. Why did I look more like the ayahs than the grownups? Why was Fairy so content to sit in Burrimummy's arms, her socks and shoes and dress and hair intact, each with bows? Why was my hair so untidy? Why didn't anyone take any notice of me? Why didn't Burrimummy dress me like she dressed Fairy?

I edge off the thakath, slip into the drawing room, and encounter the tiger's face reflected millions of times.

I see its uneven teeth reflected in infinity, in other oval gilded mirrors of various lengths around the drawing room. Burrimummy said she shot it months after she went as a bride to the Bhopal royal family. "There's nothing to tell. The tiger was drugged. I pointed and aimed and shot it. That's all."

Every inch of the walls is crammed with long mirrors endlessly reflecting photographs, of coronations, full length portraits — Burrimummy's father the Nawab of Mysore in formal regalia, with his turban and swords, Mumma Fairy, his Begum, in riding gear, sitting side-saddle; visits by the Residents; Simran with Lord Mountbatten; formal portraits of all the children of Mysore House.

I recognise some from copies in 17 Rest House Road. Here is Burrimummy dressed as a boy when she was a child, winning a fancy-dress prize. Here is Nazmeen Pasha wearing a chiffon sari and pearls, his elbows daintily perched on a mantelpiece. Here is Burrimummy, with the sheerest of saris, showing off her entire petticoat, the fairest of them all. And Mummy, a child, with a sweet oval face seated in front in a silk kurta and dupatta. I long to be part of that photograph. The mirror shows me a dark girl with short black hair and a thin body like the servants. I can spin myself into the photo in the room with tapestries and the grand piano.

I'm hearing musical voices, rising like the notes of a piano, without any discord.

Nazmeen is shouting.

"I could have had whomever I wanted. I went with father and mother to Government House where I danced with Lord Mountbatten and met Bhutto, a very handsome man. Bhutto invited us to tea at the Taj. He told Puppa he wanted to marry me, but father refused, giving some excuse about not wanting me to live in Lahore, and that was even before partition. Mumma thought father was crazy. She was furious. He was brilliant, just back from Oxford. Father said it was too late. He had already refused."

Burrimummy says, "Yes, Naimoo, but the real reason was that his mother was a dancing girl, wasn't it? Anyway, he'd be executed by now and you'd be a widow."

"Well, you know how that feels, don't you?"

Burrimummy says, "The Pakistanis like fair girls."

"Oh, go to hell, Burri Bibi. Better to be dark than twice divorced like you. What the hell have you done for anybody? We've never had ONE meal in your precious Rest House Road."

I hear Burrimummy's voice wavering between pleading and rage.

"What have I done? You've forgotten all the years I took care of Mumma?"

"Yes, you took great care of her. That's why she can't stand you. You bullied her. That's what you did."

All this time I am spinning, spreading my arms around me. I spin in front of the mirror, reflected infinitely with the tiger skin and its spreading gold and black fur, to the grand piano elegantly curved, its pedals out like paws beneath a velvet dress, with the crystal chandelier shattering with each swirl. I am spinning out of their spiteful voices into a lovely place.

I hear a noise, and rush to hide, but a big hand catches hold of me. Orange tobacco lands on my cheeks. "What is Zia's little black girl doing dancing in the drawing room like a Hindu monkey?"

It is Nazmeen with her sharp features and fierce voice. I am terrified, but know this is the wrong time to cry. She hauls me back into the veranda.

There is another scene, with Burrimummy also screaming, also hurtling chewed up betel nut juice like fire all around her.

"This is the limit. She's a small CHILD. You are the blackie, Nazmeen. YOU are."

Burrimummy grabs the eau de cologne beside Simran and says, "I'm sick of you all. I just want to DIE." I watch with alarm as she tries to drink it. Fairy starts to cry. Mamujaan restrains Burrimummy and says, "Just wait. Just wait." He returns with a shotgun and holds it to his head. "Burri Bibi, if you drink that I will SHOOT myself. I'm tired and fed up with the fights. Every time you come here, you fight."

I already know no one will die. They always behave like this.

We hear the click as he removes the safety catch and heaving with asthma holds the bore against his head.

Simran, Nazmeen, and Burrimummy start screaming.

I was black. Like the ayahs. I was a monkey. I didn't belong here. That's why I was invisible to my mother.

Burrimummy took me home and put me together piece by piece with stories that were hundreds of years old. She's YOUR great-grandmother, she said, showing me the photo of a young Mumma with a diamond in her hair. Burrimummy's mother Fairy, who married the Nawab of Mysore against her will, was mine.

FIVE POEMS

Richard Georges

LITTLE LION

For Uncle Earl, Mini-Man

One daughter says blunder to mean thunder.

Sometimes I remember my late uncle,

so-called *Mini-Man,* a diminutive

Rasta, a life lived in bush, wooden stand

filled with produce at the side of the

road in Maracas: the fruit of the season,

greens, ground provisions, an awakeness

that translates into dirt floors, tin roof,

gaps in the walls. I can't remember

him now. I only dream him, see
his stubbornness in my daughters, see his
children red as this open earth, and my
mother dissolved in despair, her heaving
grief and the mountain's echoing thunder.

Wardian Case

Like Pissarro with his Whitman beard, the scene before me,
ground doves skittering across the dusty earth, a lonely hound

moping roadside. The police assembled in their blacks and whites
standing to attention in the Old Festival Ground, the children,

dressed accordingly (scouts, guides, their neckties fixed rigidly),
and a fading Union Jack buffeting in the summer wind.

The visitors, naval officers, in their bleached costumes,
stare blankly at the green hills in the distance.

This is a view for the colonial collection
(next to the flagellating donkeys, the Negro washerwomen,

the coconut trees bowing over beaches,
and the blond sky glowing behind them).

In the moments before the drums spark up
new bodies bend and break in the old song and dance.

Perhaps I see a little girl fidgeting in a starched shirt —
yellow set against the rusting mangroves

under the straining trumpets and the lit arch of the sun
and wonder if this din is meant to carry

across the ridged waves like some clamour
from Jericho, to let them know that we are still here.

And good. Behaved. Eager to strap ourselves
into the armours of a long-dead Empire.

Burn

For Andre Bagoo

So, Brother, that light burning in the hills
like a deya is yours. The channel ripples
and stipples the light, and the moon
burns a halo into the arid sky.

This is a night full of voices:
the infant wailing at the baptismal font,
the weeping about the silent casket.
The whole damn world is alight
and hungry and nothing is ever enough —
but there is poetry, which will suffice.

ANTILIA

Look, Stranger: the night lights flicker above
the damp earth. Do you hear crickets calling?
The night things know your name, the bright stars
Echo the melancholy chorus the ground dove
sings to you — and this repeating island,
this broken bridge of your America,
interrupts itself again. And the band
playing the rhythms of this replica
reminds you what it's all about —
the echoing surf and a nameless ocean.
All was fine within and all was fine without
but for those few moments I forgot to see
the parts of the sky that cease to be sky,
like birds and other delights.

THE HISTORY (OR GEOGRAPHY) OF BAYS

by now we must all know
that the sea is made of tears

but if I squint, the lights on the yachts in the bay
look like stars, rocking to   & fro

the world seems bigger from here
from so many empty bays   & I think the only way
to survive, to drown everything within myself,

is to be as fervent as the sea —
to see the only world as the one we sing in
& bleed in. The shape of the bay

& shorelines are political;
the site of landings & departures;
of invasions and exiles;

where liquid gives way to solid —
like land eaten by the sea,   an always missing.

LETTUCE

Sharon Millar

Aidan was standing at the stove, gently prodding a large rump roast while a mushroom sauce puffed fat bubbles on the burner behind. The kitchen was hot, the heat of the day still pulsing off the walls. But, through the northern windows, a cool breeze was coming across the ridge and bringing the smell of the ylang ylang tree into the room.

"Is the meat ready?" Marguerite was screwing in the backs of her earrings as she came through the door, trailing wisps of perfume.

The kitchen was a large room lined with mahogany cupboards with tiny inserts of stained glass, an industrial stainless steel stove, and wide malachite counters. Outside in the garden, Sara and Emma were decorating the dinner table that Marguerite put on the lawn so the guests could eat under the stars. The two girls looked like Marguerite. They were placing bright pink bougainvillaea bracts along the centre of the table, the type of tropical centrepiece they knew foreigners loved.

Aidan had custom-designed the kitchen himself, throwing himself into the project after his affair ended. In the long painful months that followed the end of his affair, he'd spent his time poring over kitchen design books and drawing floor plans. He had knocked out a wall and incorporated an old storeroom, doubling the size of the kitchen. The new kitchen looked out onto the lawn, its line of sight clear to the end of the garden. He told everyone that it was his tribute to Marguerite's cooking. She was an excellent cook, a natural. From the old kitchen, a steady stream of light, flaky pastries, creamy murgh makhanis, veal marsalas, stuffed artichokes, basil pestos, chocolate mousses, and tender baby pavlovas had flowed, Marguerite's long, slim fingers rolling and kneading. There'd always been a pot, hot and fragrant, on the stove. The new kitchen, he'd said hollowly, was his tribute to her. It was what he told their friends. When they were alone, they never spoke of the kitchen.

Marguerite was not cooking tonight. It had been Aidan's idea to have the Joneses to dinner and she had gone along with the idea easily enough. There was none of the old enthusiasm, just an agreeable placidity and a refusal to cook. She wouldn't even fry an egg. Occasionally, she made cheese and toast for the girls, but generally she took them out to eat. Now she came up behind him, looking over his shoulder at the rump roast that sat on the stove. Just out of the oven, it sat leaking pink dots of blood from its surface. In the hot kitchen, Aidan stepped away from the stove to look at her face as she examined the meat. He was tired and irritated by the smell of heavy meat grease. In a thin white muslin shirt with small gold buttons and a pair of white jeans, Marguerite looked cool and fresh. He'd started cooking hours ago, enjoying a false feeling of competence, but he was not a natural cook and he'd kept calling up to her for help. Eventually she'd come downstairs and sat with him, polishing her nails while she gave instructions.

Did she know? He'd asked himself that question over and over. She'd never accused him, never given him so much as an inkling that she suspected anything. She had never asked. Not even when she'd caught him crying in front of the television set late one night. She'd simply turned around and gone back to bed.

Now Marguerite stood next to Aidan and looked at the meat. She rested her hand lightly on his shoulder as she bent over to check the meat thermometer.

"Perfect. I'd say it's done," she rubbed his back lightly as she walked away. "It's time for you to get ready. I'll light the candles and get you a drink. They'll be here in half an hour."

Aidan thinks they will make love tonight. She'd changed the sheets today and her fingers and toes winked vermillion at him as she walked away. They still made love often and he was careful not to change routines or patterns long established. She was long-bodied and flat-stomached, even after two children. Not long ago, Marguerite had surprised him in bed with a sudden moth like swoop, her hair running over his belly, her mouth opening. He'd lain back waiting for the soft wetness of her mouth but she had bitten him once before nipping her way up his stomach.

He'd invited the Joneses because Kate Jones was a new colleague. She was senior to him at the multinational oil company where they worked. It was the first time the local office had been assigned such senior legal counsel, and she was young and pretty. Very easy on the eyes. He'd never met the husband, but Kate had said he was a geologist waiting for his work permit. An amateur archaeologist as well. Like my Marguerite, he'd said. They should get on very well. Come to dinner on Saturday night. Seven-ish.

Kate Jones was sitting on the edge of the bed waiting for Dylan to finish dressing. She'd spent most of the afternoon lying in bed in a bra and panty, trying to get cool. Even though their first posting had been in Egypt, she was not accustomed to the heavy island humidity. She had not known what to expect when she'd received the Trinidad and Tobago packet from head office. But once here, she'd settled well. She enjoyed the exotic feeling of a new country. She was looking forward to meeting Aidan Davis's wife. Aidan was part of her team in the office and they often worked late, a small group of them staying behind and ordering Chinese food to finish government tenders. She liked Aidan but she'd met his type before. He talked about his wife. She had a pretty name. Marguerite. And Kate was expecting a pleasant, slightly meek housewife. Sophisticated enough for an island girl but probably provincial. Aidan talked a lot about his daughters and how much his wife liked to cook. He emitted just the slightest pulse of availability, a dim but unmistakeable signal, as relentless as that of a firefly. But, she thought to herself, there was nothing wrong in going to dinner. Nothing wrong at all. It was a good idea to get to know the locals. It would be fun.

"You look nice," she said to Dylan, catching his eye in the mirror as he buttoned his shirt.

He looked polished and handsome. It was hard to know what to wear to these dinners. He'd chosen to wear a pair of jeans and a white shirt. Simple. He's met the wife, he tells her.

"Where would you have met Marguerite Davis?" Kate was surprised he hadn't mentioned this before.

"I met her when I volunteered at the archaeological dig last month. I didn't make the connection until you said her name." He was still buttoning his shirt. "Marguerite."

Something in the way he said the other woman's name made Kate look at him more closely. Some languidness on his tongue, a subtle heaviness deep in his throat that she alone could hear.

"What's she like?"

"Tall. Striking. She studied archaeology but stayed home once she'd had the children. Now she volunteers on weekends." He paused. "She said I sounded Trinidadian, with the Welsh accent. It's similar."

Kate was careful to keep her face neutral. Now she really wanted to meet this Marguerite.

They'd been digging at the Banwari Trace site. That large shell midden on the southern edge of the Oropouche Lagoon. He was from Wales, he told her. A geologist. But his wife was the one with the job.

"Dylan Jones," he'd said, holding out his hand.

"Marguerite Davis." She'd rocked back on her heels to take off her gloves and shake his hand. It was warm and dry. She liked the way he held her hand in his palm.

"This site is famous, isn't it? I read up on it before I came."

She reached into her bag and pulled out a faded folder.

Banwari Man. The skeleton was discovered lying on its left side. In typical Amerindian fashion, it lay along the northwest axis and had been lying there for 5,400 years just 20 centimetres below the surface.

"It's the oldest archaeological site in the Caribbean." She liked that he had researched her home before he'd come. So many foreigners came and went with no sense of the island beyond what lay in the tourist brochures.

"When was the burial site found?"

"November 1969."

He whistled softly. "That puts it at . . ." he stopped to calculate. "3400 BC?" He shook his head in amazement. "That's hard to comprehend."

"You can visit him. Or her. They are not sure of the gender. I like to think of her as the first woman. So you can visit the oldest person in the Caribbean at the university museum. One of our well-kept secrets."

When she smiled, her face was opened and relaxed, making her beautiful.

"Maybe you can take me one day."

"Yes." She hesitated for a second. "Yes. I can."

She'd been just four years old in 1969, she told him. Occupying the earth for the equivalent of a breath. Just think. Thousands of years ago, someone was buried here. She did not usually talk like this, but there was something in Dylan's attention that drew the words out. They were working on a kitchen midden, carefully sifting and looking for potsherds and small bones. Clues to meals that had been prepared and served. They'd worked all day, carefully bagging and documenting small, fragile finds. She told him about the time they had come upon the remains of a cachalot whale on the Manzanilla coast. Unusual. They were accustomed to otters, manatees, and water rats. But a whale?

"Strange to imagine all the cooking that must have happened here," she said. "All the meals eaten. It's such a human thing. To eat with people. To feed the ones you love."

"Do you cook?" he'd asked.

"I used to. Not so much anymore."

It was just past four in the afternoon when the shout came down the line. That's it for the day.

They'd hugged before saying goodbye. A quick short hug.

"Don't forget you have to take me to see Banwari Man," he'd said over his shoulder as he walked towards his car.

"I won't," she said. "See you soon."

She took the long way home, coming back via Mayaro and Manzanilla, wanting to see the ocean. Here at the Ortoire River was the gentle swing onto the main road that passed the fishermen hawking red fish and lobster. And soon the crisscrossing of wavelets where the Nariva River ran into the Atlantic. In the old days, Marguerite would have stopped for lobsters, but Aidan did the cooking now and he didn't know how to cook lobster.

Aidan was relieved the food was out of the way. It had gone better than he imagined. The roast was perfect. The potatoes not overdone and the broccoli salad not too wet. The introductions had gone well but he'd been surprised to find that Marguerite and Dylan knew each other.

"Why didn't you tell me you'd met him?" he whispered, catching her in the kitchen.

"I didn't make the connection," she said. "Honestly, I was just as surprised as you."

He knew her well enough to see she was lying.

"Hurry, it's time to get the dessert on the table." And with that, she was out the door, bright and smiling.

"A toast to the chef," said Marguerite, raising her red wine high. "And a toast to new friends. Welcome to Trinidad."

When Aidan looked at her, she was flushed even though she'd had only two glasses of wine.

"Yes, a toast," said Kate. "To many more dinners on your beautiful island."

"Have you enjoyed it so far?" Marguerite poured herself another glass of wine.

When Marguerite looked up, Kate was looking directly at her with an unreadable expression on her face. Dylan sat to the right of Marguerite but he was turned away from her now, his attention apparently on Aidan, but both women could tell he was listening closely to the conversation.

"It's very different to Egypt. Out there we had moonlight dinners in the desert. It was all very romantic with the pyramids and all that. It just seems harder to get out in Trinidad."

Marguerite smiled at the other woman. "Trinidad is very beautiful. We were once joined to South America."

There was a subtle challenge in Marguerite's voice. A mere hint of competition. Kate looked at her more closely. Marguerite made it sound as if Egypt were a dry barren place compared to . . . Compared to what? To Marguerite? To this little island spit on the edge of the continent?

As if tuned to his wife's voice, Aidan directed his attention to the women. They seemed connected by a glittery jangly energy.

From where he sat, Marguerite was all hard angles. All jawline and collarbone. Sitting among the familiar, Aidan had a vertiginous moment, a sudden sense of shift. From where they sat, the dining room was still the same space. Nothing had changed. His stone floors and coral walls. They ate in the garden just beyond the open French doors, light and shadow stitching the grass around them into a tapestry of deep moss and grasshopper green. From outside the house, the living room was framed by the large plate window. From the garden, the living room glowed softly in the dim light, its soft lumps of cushions and low couches assuring him that this was still his home, his wife, his children.

Aidan had not known this world as a child. He had come from a home of hard shapes and spaces. Dark corners and small windows. Everything about his parents' home had been sparse. Not that there was no money. Rather, there had been an almost puritanical sense of meanness served up as frugality. All excess was frowned upon as self-indulgence. It was all, he understood much later, self-righteous pride of their Church of England decorum in the face of the overblown hysteria of Roman Catholicism and the excessive breeding of the French Creoles.

His people had been in the Caribbean for some two hundred years. British stock who had remained bankers, accountants, clerks. Efficient at bureaucracy. Marguerite's mixed Martinique background could be traced back to the 1700s. A long laundry list of ancestors — coloured planters with their own slaves, Royalists fleeing revolution, a high ranking British lawyer who had thirteen children before leaving his wife for a young Polish widow. There was even a branch of her family that had come from Venezuela to work the cocoa. Cocoa Panyols. Some of her sisters were blonde and blue-eyed but Marguerite was olive with the thick, smooth skin of Mediterranean blood. There was even an unexplored Haitian connection. There was no end of compartments to Marguerite. Her world had seemed rooted and beautiful to him and he had grafted himself onto her as easily as a lime mossed onto an orange tree. These things were impossible to explain to foreigners and they had long given up with explanations. They were here and there was nowhere else to call home.

For months he'd been waiting for the confrontation. The accusations. Some sign of hysteria. But she was the same Marguerite, except she now closed the bathroom door to shower and she'd stopped cooking. It was as if she was methodically making her way around herself and locking each compartment away. Easily and quietly. But still he waited for the ball to drop.

Marguerite's tone had caught his attention and for a moment he wondered if she had saved it all up for a moment such as this. Would she challenge his colleague? His boss really, truth be told. Would she dare? He watched her carefully as she looked at Kate. Her full attention was on Kate and the mongoose-like concentration was not an expression he had ever seen on her face.

Kate shifted suddenly in her seat. She leaned in and whispered something to Marguerite behind a cupped hand. There was nervous whispering from Kate and then a reassuring smile from Marguerite.

"Come." Marguerite rose to her feet and Kate followed her up the stairs.

Kate stood behind Marguerite in the bathroom while Marguerite opened her medicine cabinet.

"Here you are..." Marguerite said. "Saved by the tampon. Are you sure you don't want to borrow a change of clothes?"

"No, I'm fine. Caught it in time. I've had cramps all day, I should have guessed."

The tension dissipated over the box of tampons and now the two women stood in the close space of the bathroom. Kate could smell the intimate smell of the other woman. An undertone of talcum powder and a cat-like muskiness. There was Marguerite's nightie hanging on the back of the door. Kate had one very similar. White muslin with embroidered roses around the hem. Kate relaxed and softened, the safe domesticity of another woman's space comforting and lulling her.

"Shout if you need anything." Marguerite pulled in the door and Kate could hear her disappearing down the stairs.

They used the same brand of tampon. This seemed like a sign to Kate. Maybe this woman would be a friend after all.

She washed her hands in the sink and looked at herself in the mirror. She was flushed from the two glasses of wine. She reapplied her lipstick, smiled at her reflection, and opened the medicine cabinet. Marguerite's medicine cabinet was very neat. Kate thought that said a lot about the woman. A bottle of Advil, a pack of plasters, a small box of birth control, and a nail file. Beige Number 2 face powder and three lipsticks in varying shades of red. Tucked behind the bottle of Advil was a picture of a much younger Aidan and Marguerite holding hands. Downstairs, she could hear that someone had turned up the music.

In the garden, the table had been cleared. Kate ran into Marguerite coming into the kitchen with a vase of hanging heliconias.

"From your garden? They're lovely."

"Snake in the balisier!" Aidan had followed Marguerite in with the last few dishes.

"What an expression." Kate looked at the pendulous flowers with a new eye.

"Don't listen to him. He's just rattling your cage. It's an old political expression. Meaningless unless you live here."

"Who is this, Marguerite? She's so striking." Kate picked up a silver-framed photograph of an older woman. The woman sat slightly left of centre, her eyes and attention caught by something off-camera. In the black and white photograph, she was dressed in Victorian clothing. Other than that, she could have been Marguerite. She even wore her hands. The same long fingers and delicate wrists.

A gold band circled her wrist. Kate recognised both the bracelet and the wedding ring. A thin band of gold with a single diamond. She'd admired both on Marguerite earlier.

"Here you go." Marguerite stretched her hands out, the Merlot glowing garnet in thin crystal, the gold on her wrist sitting there as if she'd been born with it. Kate looked at her as if she were a ghost. Perhaps she had had too much to drink. Looking from the woman in the frame to the woman before her, Kate felt caught between the two women.

"My great-grandmother. They say I look like her."

"That's an understatement. Did you know her?"

"No, my grandfather was her last child. She had thirteen in all. All home births." Marguerite shook her head. "Imagine that. Placentas in buckets and all the rest."

"What happened to her?"

"My great-grandfather was a lawyer. He left her for a young Polish widow when my grandfather was a baby. A chance meeting in Port of Spain. The widow was beautiful and injured. Some combination. She was on her way to Venezuela with her parents. She'd hurt herself during the crossing. When they stopped in Trinidad, the ship's captain brought her to my great-grandfather to write her will."

"And?"

"She recovered. Fell in love with my much older great-grandfather. He went with her to Venezuela and had two more children. Both girls." Here she stopped and looked at the photograph again. "Imagine that. A random meeting. So many lives changed."

Kate was silent. She took the photo from Marguerite and looked at the woman again. She looked at her hands, at the abalone brooch at her neck. Thirteen children and the man leaves you. Just like that.

"So interesting." What else could she say?

"That's one way to look at it. Come, let's go find the men. Enough stories." Marguerite smiled and reached out for Kate, the gold band and the slim wedding ring glowing softly against her skin.

"Why do you wear her ring?"

"I only started wearing it a few months ago. I felt for a change, I guess. Come, let's go and have some fun."

On the table, the great-grandmother sat with her abalone brooch, glancing off to the side.

"Let's dance!" Aidan was mixing another whiskey and soda on the table and wondering if it was safe to start flirting with Kate.

"Why don't we?" Kate clapped her hands. "It's been so long."

"Let's turn off the lights."

"I'm going to check on the children," Marguerite said. "Make sure everyone is down for the night before we start our debauchery."

Everything was fine, thought Aidan. It's going better than I imagined. And he would get to dance with Kate. What was some harmless flirting?

"Where is Dylan? Kate suddenly looked around. "I haven't seen him since I came down."

"He's out on the patio, looking at the moon."

They smiled at each other. See? It was all harmless.

On the way back down the stairs, Marguerite ran into Dylan.

"Hi, I was looking for Kate."

"Oh Dylan, she's fine. She's back downstairs. She's in the garden with Aidan. They're making plans for dancing."

The dim light of the stairs made it difficult to read his face. He stood on the step below her looking up. Quietly he reached out and stroked the side of her face and then ran his fingers lightly across her lips. Sliding past him on the narrow stairway, she allowed her breasts to press against his chest.

Inside, Marguerite pushed back the couch and lit a few candles. At first, they all danced on their own. Singing out loud. Stamping the ground. The playlist veered between calypso, old dub, some classic rock. Soon the tempo changed, slowed, and bit by bit the couples shifted around each other. First they danced with their spouses and then they switched.

Aidan and Kate flirted with gusto. Lots of flamboyant gestures, spinning and dipping. It was some time before they noticed Marguerite and Dylan, dancing quietly and closely in a corner of the room. They danced near the window with a courtly decorum. In Dylan's arms, Marguerite moved like liquid silver. There was no more dipping and flirting from the other two and when the song finished, Aidan turned on the lights and pushed the couch back into place. Kate went and stood at Dylan's side.

"I'm ready to go." She looked down at her hands. "The food was wonderful. Thank you so much." She stopped for a moment and looked over at Marguerite. "Did you cook? Aidan always says what a good cook you are. He talks so much about building the kitchen for you." Her face was open and hurt. Dylan had it coming to him once they got in the car. But even as she thought of what she would say to him, she was suddenly afraid.

Marguerite smiled and shrugged. "I was a good cook. I am a good cook. But I just got tired one day. Aidan cooks now."

"Don't go." Aidan was desperate to save the evening. It had unravelled quickly. "Let's go onto the lawn and have one for the road."

"Yes," said Marguerite. "One for the road."

"Sounds good." Dylan was in good spirits.

In the garden, they sat in silence. Marguerite sat in the shadow of the jacaranda tree, which shed purple flowers in a corolla of violet around her chair. Her hair was pulled back from her face with a wide black band exposing a brow as smooth and calm as that of a child. She lit a cigarette, pulling it out of a small silver case. Aidan watched her hold the smoke deep in her lungs before expelling a long lavender plume. He wanted to slap her.

"I no longer cook but I still grow vegetables," Marguerite said suddenly, stubbing and extinguishing the cigarette in a silver ashtray. "Come, I'll show you."

The three followed her around the side of the house and through the latticed side gate that opened onto a small terraced patch. From here, the side of the garden sloped away and the city was again spread out before them. Marguerite grew yellow and red sweet peppers, tomatoes, long pendulous purple eggplants, and small, upright, lightly furred ochroes, some of which lay on the ground, split to reveal tiny pink pods. There was also basil and fennel, rosemary and mint. But it was her lettuce that took up most of the plot. Row upon row of flawless, ribbed leaves. Some had opened wide and lay with their leaves spread back, older and darker green, revealing the pale, tender hearts, with puckered surfaces. Others were still young and closed, the frilled leaves tightly clenched over hidden centres.

Dylan moved in front of Kate and followed Marguerite down a narrow path, making it impossible for the other two to fit in the tight space. From where they stood at the edge of the small path, Kate and Aidan could see the dark heads of their spouses in the dim light. Marguerite broke a leaf of lettuce. She bent and snapped it from the centre of a young plant, pulled it from the heart where the tiny fronds were curly and delicate and green. Before Kate could call out, Marguerite had fed Dylan the leaf.

"Dylan!" Kate's voice carried an edge of desperation. "You can't just eat lettuce from the ground like that. You'll get sick. Dylan! Stop! Stop!"

They could hear the panic in her voice as she pushed her way past Aidan and down the narrow path. She pulled Dylan away, tugging him hard and pinching the soft underside of his arm.

"It's okay, Kate." Aidan was next to them, reaching for his wife. "He's fine. It's okay."

Back in the kitchen, Kate stayed close to Dylan. She tried to make a joke about eating unwashed lettuce, giving a complicated story about getting sick in Mexico after eating local salad.

"Don't you remember, Dylan?" She was still trying to reclaim lost ground. "You were dreadfully ill. We almost didn't get on the plane. You never know, when you're in a strange country." She paused after this, flushed and sweating, a red wash coming up from between her breasts and rising in spotty patches up her neck. Marguerite and Dylan were silent.

"We've been sick as well on holiday, haven't we, Marguerite?" Aidan had the extraordinary sensation of standing at the edge of a cliff, a tinny, hollow feeling of loss that he was unable to pinpoint. It was only a lettuce leaf, he wanted to say.

Marguerite packed a bag of vegetables for them to take home. Her face was guileless and fresh.

"Bye," she said. "You must come again."

"We will," said Dylan. "If I don't see you on a dig before."

Aidan saw Kate pinch her husband hard. Her face began to crumble in the centre and she turned and left without looking at Marguerite.

After he'd locked up downstairs, Aidan came into their bedroom. Marguerite had bathed and lay on her side away from him. Her hair was wet and she'd combed it back so it shone as dark and slick on her head as an otter's pelt. He was very angry and not a little drunk but when she turned to him in the silver light of the room and opened her arms, he went to her willingly. Tonight he would unlock her, he would show her. She was supple and pliable, compliant and loving.

"Why?" he whispered. "Tell me why? What's wrong with you?"

But she answered with an open mouth and a smooth thigh and he knew why. When he turned over to sleep, Aidan convinced himself he had saved his marriage. Now they were even.

Next to him Marguerite lay quietly, her otter head wetting the pillow. She imagined the water in the gulf rising. She imagined crevices and hidden caves and steep slopes; slatey phyllites and pleats of metamorphic rock. Silts, and gravels with their seepages of crude oil. She turned onto her stomach, enjoying the movement of her body. She wondered when she would see the Welsh man again. She lay until Aidan's even breathing told her he was asleep. Quietly she made her way through the still house, through the beautiful kitchen. Even in the dim light, the counters and appliances gleamed, everything in its place. But there was nothing of her here. She would never cook here again.

All anyone remembered was the young Polish widow who stepped off a gangplank one bright Tuesday en route to Venezuela.

Banwari man. The skeleton was discovered lying on its left side. In typical Amerindian fashion, it lay along the northwest axis and had been lying there for 5,400 years just 20 centimetres below the surface.

There was so little of a life. In the end, it was all gone. The malachite counters, the stone floors, the coral walls. All that mattered were the people you chose to feed.

Marguerite knew the poem by heart.

Split seam and thirteen
Polish widows fall like rain
A gangplank to Port of Spain
Says the amethyst to the thirteen
Father gave me over in good faith
The excess and the break

A splendid day to be ill
Says the mother of pearl
The lawyer furiously scribbles
And it is done

The Naparimas weep
Far away from the gangplank
But still
The Polish bride is young and beautiful

The amethyst and mother of pearl
Thirteen grown from San Fernando
Do not know Poland
The wedding ring replaced
By a black band

It all ends in Maracaibo.

Out in the garden, she sat for a long time, the jacaranda slowly
shedding slivers of violet.

FOUR POEMS

Peta-Gaye Williams

When You Eat a Mango

Before you eat a mango, peel it with your eyes,
let your senses sink into the sweetness of its soul.
Inhale, feel the magic moving through your veins,
watch a *julie* in its splendour, take a *beefy* for a bite,
sweetie come brush me, tender and ripe.

Hold a stringy mango, best to eat that one at nights
when maggots fade under the cover of dark.
Take a *bombay mango,* hold it in your hand,
feel the firmness between your fingers, slice into its gut,
scoop the inside out, feel it melting in your mouth.

Pause, then bite into its flesh, flavours

floating steady on your tongue like an oasis of tastes and scents.

Watch the juices slide in between your fingers

cascading down your palm like liquid gold

sticky and sweet. An' wen yuh done,

lick di juices from your hand like freedom.

HOLDING

I wish I had a man to hold my hand,
my father never did, all my life
I've only known the touch
of mothers, grandmothers, and aunts.

I learned to cook just like grandmother,
to change a tyre the same way too,
all my lessons on boys and babies
came from my mother's point of view.

I wish there was a fist to rescue,
to rush to my defence,
and a shoulder broad and steady
for the days when things get tense.

I wish I had a man to hug me,
my father never did,
but in my dreams somewhere between
fantasy and need

he washes my hair with aloe vera,
puts lotion on my skin,

oils my scalp, ties ribbons, clips,
walks with me to school,
puts my pink lunch bag on his shoulder
and sports it like it's cool.

He tells me to be different,
calls me princess before I sleep,
says it's okay to be my own self
my own versions of me.

I wish this man would touch me,
hold me in his sight, wrap me
in the warm assurance of a hug,
soothe me in the comfort of his love.

Submissive

I let you adjust me in your arms for a change
No one ever did that to me before
I was always doing the holding
My last lover called it controlling

I let you put the sweetness inside me for a change
At first when you touched me it felt so strange
to be on the other side of a touch, floating
helplessly in the unknown

It all sounds different when someone else plays,
you hear in between melodies a silence that says
constellations are going to collide
you feel it building up on the inside

a tide that goes slowly and comes
running perpendicular to my truth
breaking, bending in your arms
numb with the sweetness inside me for a change

TEMPTATION, PERSUASION, SEDUCTION

Temptation
is you watching me steam in the desire and lust
that boils in my blood for you,
seeing me simmering down like a stew
feeling the heat, having the desire to put out the flame,
knowing the longing that lingers in places you can't see
knowing that what I feel for you
is no more than a fleeting reality
tilting your head in the direction of sin
but walking away before it sucks you in.

Persuasion
is me insisting you should stay
convincing you to do it anyway
for right is a state of mind
and wrong is a cause, my cause
worthy of being pursued

Seduction
is you watching my body leaving my soul
watching my body losing control
watching me lead my body to an imminent death,

breath steadily leaving my whole

depth deeper than the secrets I hold.

Frustration is you leaving me still untouched.

DEAR DEPARTED

Hazel Simmons-McDonald

I

Albertina Toussaint walked along the narrow path between the rows of graves in the cemetery. She smiled, thinking the cemetery was set out almost like the streets of the city with the paths crossing each other and creating distinct blocks. The next block over from where she stood would take her to the row with Cyril's grave. She muttered as she walked. It's like walking from Grass Street to Mary Ann Street and just like how our houses used to be. Ours on Grass Street and his on Mary Ann Street. She pursed her lips as she remembered Cyril. I will leave a candle for you so you can rest in peace. She walked towards the row with Cyril's grave. It was All Souls' Day and the cemetery was aglow with the flickering flames of candles and small battery-operated lamps that families and friends had placed on the graves of their loved ones. Albertina stopped and checked the bag which she held in one hand and which contained candles, a couple small vases, bottles, and a box of matches. In her other hand she clutched a few bunches of flowers which had already started to wilt. She closed the bag and continued along the path. I didn't forget nothing this time. I going to Cyril first. After all, he was my husband. Even though I didn't see him for most of the years we married.

She walked between two graves, sat down on one and placed her bags on it. She was short of breath. After a while she opened the bag, took out a vase, put a bunch of flowers in it, and poured some water from one of the bottles in the bag. Look what nice flowers I bring for you, Cyril. I bring some pink roses because you used to like them and some ferns to finish the bouquet. I sure that will make you happy. This year I bring a lamp with a shade. It have batteries so it will continue to light when the candle burn down. So you getting one candle and one lamp. I sure you will like that too. She lit the candle and turned on the lamp. She stood up and tilted her head to one side. The grave looking real nice, you know. See how it paint up and your name clear on the headstone. I sure that making you happy. I wish all this happiness was there before you get here, though. We didn't even have a chance to talk before you get here. Eh eh! They bring you home in a box, a big present for me, cold like ice, not a word and I there waiting for you to walk in the door. Eh eh! That wasn't nice. She took another bottle from the bag, unscrewed the top and took a swig from the bottle. She wiped her mouth with the back of her hand, took another swig, screwed the cap on, and put the bottle back in the bag. That is what keep me warm all these years, you know; that and Alphonse. Don't get vex now. Is you who leave me. I sit down waiting, my face getting gwiji, crease up like a ole prune. What's that you say? Listen, I not getting in any long talk now, you hear? Look how the place pretty. Look how your grave light up and nice. Rest in peace, you hear? I goin round by Alphonse grave to put some flowers for him. I sure his children leave already so I can go and put a little remembrance for him too. You don't have to get vex. What's that you say? Pa alé? Don't go? Why I must not go? Like you talking to me all de time now? Your voice runnin in my head like the rara de children start to make already for Christmas. Listen, you is dust in there, you know. But see how the flowers looking nice in the light. I going now.

She gathered the other flowers, picked up her bag, and set off slowly down the row. It getting late, you know. I had to wait until Alphonse children left because I ain't want to meet them here. I will put a light and flowers for him. They ent going come back here for another year, so they ent going know who put them there. Everything will be gone by next year except the candle wax and they not going remember what they put here for him. Cyril mus be blue vex because I putting flowers and candle for Alphonse. But why he have to be vex? He die well before Alphonse come by me. Eh eh, sa pou fè? What to do? She walked up to a grave which had two lighted lamps and a couple wreaths on it. My, my! They treat you nice this year, they treat you real nice, but I suppose one lamp and one wreath is for you and the other ones is for your madam. I sure she won't mind if I put this little bunch of flower and a candle for you. I have to tell you thanks but I sorry for the shame too.

She placed the vase with the flowers between the wreaths, lit a candle, made the sign of the cross and turned away. Madam, don be vex; I praying for you . . . what's dat you say, Alphonse? I sure I hear you say it don't matter just like you use to tell me. It don matter? The priest tell me I must pray for her too so I doin that, and I was jus telling she about that when you interrupt me. Look how nice my flowers and candle looking right there between your wreath and she own. She reached into the bag, took out the small flask, unscrewed the cap, and took a long drink.

It cold here, you know, even with all these lights I feeling cold right in my stomach. She started to walk away then stopped and turned back to look at the grave. What you say, Alphonse? Stay? I stay long enough already. The madam ain't goin like it if I sit down on de grave talking with you and she inside there too. Same like I hearing you, she mus be hearing everyting we saying. I feel enough shame for you already so I goin now. She walked away mumbling and gesticulating as she moved towards the entrance of the cemetery. She felt a hand on her shoulder and cried out, "Bon Dyé!" She turned round quickly.

"My God, you make me jump. I didn hear you."

"Miss Albertine, you OK?" Her neighbour, Juliana, was peering at her with a worried look. "I saw you talking and waving your hands as though something was bothering you."

"Is nothing, Julie; sé pa anyen. I okay. Is jus my head full up . . . they talking to me all de time . . . telling me all sorta ting. Is nothing."

"Who? Who talking to you?" Juliana looked around then back at Albertine. "Who telling you what?"

Albertine pushed up her glasses from the tip of her nose and stared at Juliana. "Never mind, you wouldn understand."

"I can give you a lift if you want. The car is parked over there. I have to make one quick stop and I'll be back in a few minutes."

"Thanks, I'll wait for you." Albertine walked slowly towards the cars parked at the entrance. Don bother follow me, you hear? Go back; is here you belong.

Juliana dropped her off at her house and watched as Albertine went inside. The house remained dark for a long while and she thought to follow Albertine to make sure she was fine, but just as she was about to turn off the engine a light came on inside and she drove off.

II

Cyril

Albertine sat at the small kitchen table. Her shoulders were hunched, her elbows propped on the table, and she cradled her head in the palms of her hands. The naked bulb at the end of a long cord hanging from the ceiling cast a glow on a covered shoebox on the table in front of her. She looked up, reached for the flask next to the box, drank from it and shook her head. No, I say no, is not me who cause all dat. Is not me, is Cyril. She removed the lid from the box and took out a dried spray of flowers. The jasmine still smelling sweet. They still here, sweet like when Cy did give me. She reached into the box and picked up a bundle of letters tied together with a faded red ribbon. She took out another bundle tied loosely with a blue ribbon, then she reached in and took out a single envelope. She ran her finger along the top edge and placed it next to the other two bundles on the table. She untied the ribbon from the first bundle and spread the letters in front of her. She picked up one, pulled a couple sheets of paper from the envelope, held them up to the light, pushed her glasses up from the tip of her nose, and started to read. Every now and then she read aloud.

"I must tell you, Tina, this place not the best to live. You wouldn't like it. Is like a camp. The house I living in have only one bedroom and a small kitchen and bathroom. I know if you was here that would be a paradise for me, but I out every day, for most of the day, and you wouldn't like that. Is a place for people to work and then leave when the work finish. That's what I will do, my dear. Soon as I make enough money to buy a bigger house, I will leave here and come home. I does think about you all the time, I really missing you. I can't wait to come back. Your one true love, Cy."

She hummed softly as she folded the letter and put it back in the envelope. She stopped humming, tilted her head sharply to the left, a slight frown on her brow. What you say, Cy? You still love me? Is now you telling me? Why you didn' take me with you? Why you didn' come back sooner, eh? Why? She reached for the flask and took a long drink. Ahh, dat warm me up. Is only dat I have now, you know. Don't bother me, Cy. Not because I reading your letters you must think you should come to bother me. You hear what I tell you? You leave me and gone, what you expect? Is not me to blame, you hear? She picked up another letter, pushed her glasses up from the tip of her nose, and started to read.

"My Tina, your letter arrived safely and I read it over and over. I miss you too, my dear, and I will come home soon, don't you worry. The girl who does come to clean the house saw me holding your letter to my heart and she tell me she wish she had somebody to love her like that. Did I tell you? The company send somebody to come and clean for us. Lena is the person cleaning. I will tell you more the next time I write. Take care of you for me till I come home. Your one love, Cy."

Albertine folded the letter, put it back in the envelope and placed it on the table.

Cy, is this Lena why you decide to stay over there, not so? I know everything now, even if you didn' write it out, Cy. I shoulda listen to my mind and go over there right after I get this letter. What's dat you say? It wasn't necessary? It was well necessary, you hear? But like they say, hindsight is twenty-twenty vision. She pulled the second bundle of letters towards her, took one out close to the bottom of the bundle, smoothed out the single sheet, and read.

"Dear Tina, you don't know how sorry I am I could not come for Christmas. I know you saying I broke my promise, but they had a big order to fill and the Manager ask some of us to work over the holidays. He say they would pay us double so I stay because of the extra I could make. I almost have enough for us to buy a new house. I already send a little money for you to put in the bank. Write and tell me when you get it. Is real hard working in the oilfield, Tina. They had us out there all day long over the holidays. The Manager give a party for us at the end of the work. It wasn't bad, it had dancing and everything. I learn how to dance the meringue — I will teach you when I come home. Lena, the girl who does the cleaning, show me how to dance it. I buy a few 45s to bring home. We will dance and have a good time. Take care of yourself and we will see each other soon. Your Cy."

Albertina put the letter back in the envelope. If it was only meringue you was dancing, Cy. If is only meringue things would be different. Is not what I thinking? What it was, then? Tell me. What make you stay longer and longer before you send me a letter, eh? I use to get one every two weeks, and after the holidays and the dancing I only hearing from you every two months. What is that eh? Is the meringue and the other dancing you start to do, Cy. That's what it was. But how a man can be so, eh? She sighed, picked up the last letter in the second bundle, opened it and started to read.

"Dear Tina, I writing to let you know I coming home. I book a passage on the *Lady Joy* and it leaving here the first of the month. I will be home a week after that. I coming home. Things getting a little complicated over here and I have to come home to clear my head and see you again. I make enough money for now. I will teach you to dance the meringue. We will have a party and a nice time, Tina. I want to see you again and I coming home in two weeks. Take care till I come, you hear? Cyril."

Albertina covered her face with her hands and rocked from side to side, humming softly. She lifted her head and tilted it to one side as though listening. It wasn't your fault? Not your fault? Whose fault it was, Cy? Is not me who make you change your mind. Not me. Why you had to cancel your ticket to come home? Imagine, the *Lady Joy* sail in and I there on the wharf dress up like a Christmas tree and waiting for you to come down. How you think I feel when they tell me you cancel your ticket? Eh? How you think I feel? And is not even you who tell me. You don't even write to tell me you cancelling de ticket. I don't know why you do that, Cy. What you say? You didn't cancel it, you just postpone it? For what? Miss Lena didn't want you to leave, Cy? Don't tell me not to say that, because I saying it. I saying it because it true. What difference it make? Cancel or postpone, you still ain't come, and when two months pass I still ain't hear from you and is your coffin dat arrive later. I hear Miss Lena say you was dancing when you get a heart attack. Is meringue or what, Cy? Is in de bed you was dancing? What I hear again is something you eat dat give you bad indigestion and bring on de heart attack. Is something she cook for you, Cy? She cook for you so she could keep you, not so? She picked up the last letter from the table, took out a cablegram and another sheet of paper. She opened the cable.

"Cyril fell ill last night. Did not recover. Letter follows."

She drank from the flask on the table, opened the other sheet of paper and read.

"Dear Mrs Toussaint, It is with sadness that we write to inform you of the sudden death of Mr Cyril Toussaint. He suffered a heart attack a few days before he was due to leave. An ambulance was called as soon as his helper reported that he was ill but the doctors were not able to revive him. We will be sending his body home and we will let you know of the arrangements we will be making to send his belongings. Please accept our condolences. Yours sincerely, Andre Valdez, Manager."

She reached for the flask, took a drink, and folded the letter. Is you drive me to this, Cy, is you. Alphonse help me forget. I don't know why you talking to me anyway, making me read your letters to bring all this up again. I not going to do this again, you hear? Why you even talking to me, I don know. Go back, Cy, go back to your grave and leave me alone. I gone through enough already. Maybe is de letters I keep for so long and reading once a year that making you think you can talk to me. You don't have to explain nothing, you hear? You six feet deep and is there you staying. Is enough now. I going burn the letters so I don't have to go back on these things. What you say? No, I ain't going forget you. I will put flowers and a candle for you every November, on All Souls' Day so you will rest in peace. But I not going to have conversation with you again, you hear? Is time for you to leave me, Cy.

She took another drink from the bottle, gathered the pile of letters, took a coal pot from under the kitchen sink, put the letters in it, and poured rum from her bottle on the pile. She held up one sheet, lit a match, dropped it in the coal pot, and smiled. She sat down, took another drink and started to hum and sway as she watched the letters go up in flames. She wiped tears from her cheek, rested her head on her arms and fell asleep.

III

Alphonse

There was a knock on the kitchen door. Albertine closed the tap, wiped her hands on her apron and went quickly to open the door. Her husband's friend, Alphonse, stood there. "Alphonse, is you! When you come back?"

"Morning, Bertina. I got back two days ago but I couldn't come to see you right away. So many things to settle. But I had to come because I know how bad you must be feeling about Cyril."

"You can say that again. Come in, Alphonse. I was making breakfast, saltfish with cucumber souse, and bakes. I have avocado too. You want some?"

"Thanks, Bertina, I won't say no to that."

They sat at the table, Albertina smiled as she watched Alphonse wolf down his food.

"This is good, you know. Over there in the oilfield canteen they served fish every day and sometimes chicken, but never saltfish like how we make it here. And the food wasn't highly season so you could taste the freshness of the fish. Cyril use to say they take it from the sea and throw it straight in the pot. After a while he stop eating the canteen food. He say, after your good cooking he couldn't digest that." They laughed.

"At least he remember something good I use to do. So where he use to eat then?"

Alphonse paused, looked down at his plate then looked up at Albertina. He reached out and put his hand over hers.

"Bertina, life was hard over there, real hard. Cyril was missing you bad. A day wouldn't pass without him saying how he miss you and wish he could go home."

"At first, yes, Alphonse. I believe that because he use to say it in his letters. But after a while is like he forget and the letters get cold, like he draw away from me. I sure you notice something too, but you ain't going tell me. You his friend. Where you say he was eating?"

"He pay the cleaner, Lena, to cook. He give her extra to prepare a meal for him once or twice a week and other times he cook for himself."

"So she did take over for true."

"Don't fret yourself, Bertina. It don't matter now. She never move in de house with Cyril. I never see her living there. She use to cook and I know Cyril appreciate the little she use to do."

"You all the same. Even now you covering up for Cyril. You think I don't know? Long time I suspect he had something with this Lena. He write and tell me things was getting complicated so he coming home. I believe he get in deep with she and then he decide he should leave but he cancel the trip and next thing you know, he dead. You know what happen, Alphonse, but you not goin to tell me."

"I know how you feeling, Bertina. I know is hard, but I will tell you. Lena get close to Cyril and he tell me she want him to marry her. That's when he decide to leave and come back home. Cyril couldn't carry on with that and go on like you didn't exist. He tell Lena that he was married and he had to come home to settle things. He say he didn't tell her more because you never know what could happen. He tell me he was making preparations to leave the company for good, but he didn't tell Lena that. All of that must be the complications he tell you about. Anyway, is hard to keep secret in a place like that. I think Lena must hear Cyril don't plan to return to the company."

"So is obeah she put on him to make him change his mind? Why he didn't come on the *Lady Joy* like he plan to do?"

"I don't know, Bertina. He say he had to clear up his business and he wouldn't have time to make it on the *Lady Joy*, but he was planning to leave on the next boat that come in. He tell me that and I believe him. But you know what happen."

"Yes, I know. If is true is heart attack he did have then is break his heart break to leave this Lena. I sure she put obeah on him."

"Cyril make up his mind to come home and because he know he leaving for good he say he will have a cook up and some drinks for all ah we before he leave. He say Lena offer to cook. I remember that night well. We eat and drink and have a good time, but I find it strange she give him his plate of food special. She bring it from the kitchen and give it to him. He wink at me and he eat it all up. I stay with him for a bit after the others leave and Lena say she have something to do so she going but she will return to clean up. I left when she get back. I was just going to bed when I hear a knocking on the door and is Lena there telling me come quick because Cyril pass out. When I go over there, I see Cyril on the bed. He ain't moving and he sweating. I tell Lena call for help and the ambulance came and take him to the hospital, but they say he dead by the time he get there. They say it look like he did have a heart attack but I don't know what bring that on. You ask me, Bertina, so I telling you like how it happen."

"Cyril was a sweet man. I sure Lena didn't want him to leave. If is obeah she do, must be one of dem potions they does sell that she give him. People does buy them because of the name but who know what they put in the bottle? I hear it have one they calling 'Man-U-

Must' and another one 'Leave Me Never'. Must be one of them she give him."

Alphonse stood up and placed his hands on her shoulders. "I don't know, Bertina. You can call on me anytime if you need help. I know how hard this must be for you. I will come by to visit to make sure things okay."

He left, and Bertina continued with her life of aloneness, thinking about the circumstances Cyril faced and embellishing the story Alphonse told her to her satisfaction. She made it a ritual to go to the cemetery on All Souls' Day to place flowers on his grave and light a candle. Alphonse dropped by to see her, occasionally at first; then on his way back from his early morning walks he would call out to her and she would shout an acknowledgment from wherever she was in the house. As this became something of a routine, she decided to sit by the window in the front room so they would not have to shout. He would pause by the window to ask her how she was getting on and they would talk about this and that. The pauses became visits in the front room, then coffee at the kitchen table. The friendly arm around her shoulders as he left became affectionate hugs, and one morning the rain began to pour as he was about to leave, and the hug turned into an embrace that left them clinging to each other and surrendering to a passion that left Albertina sighing as she struggled to fasten the buttons on her blouse while Alphonse pulled on his sneakers and ran out into the rain.

She did not see him for two weeks, during which time she vowed never to let herself get in such a situation again, even as she flushed with pleasure at the memory of Alphonse swearing love for her as his lips and hands found every erogenous spot on her body. Then one morning, as she lay in her bed before dawn, she heard a tapping on the kitchen door. There was Alphonse in his running clothes on his way out for his walk.

"I had to come, Bertina." She opened the door and without a

word she held his hand and led him to her still warm bed. So their affair began in earnest. They never mentioned Marie, Alphonse's wife. It was as if they alone existed in this pre-dawn world. This went on for months, and Albertine's reliance on her favourite rum diminished a little. She allowed herself a ti ponche — the local spiced rum aperitif — before lunch every day, and another one or two in the evening before going to bed. Alphonse's presence in her life and his lovemaking, though limited to the early morning visits, gave her a new lease on life, and the feeling that she was needed and loved. She was surprised one afternoon when she heard his familiar knock on her kitchen door. She opened the door and he slipped in and pulled the door shut, looking furtively behind him as he did so.

"What happen, Alphonse?"

He pulled a chair and sat at the kitchen table.

"I didn't want to stand at your front door in the middle of the day, Bertina. I think people talking enough already."

"What you mean? Who talking?"

"Marie tell me how somebody tell her I coming here in the morning. She say I making a pappyshow and a bétise with she life. She say the neighbours looking at her and laughing and she not going to let nobody make her look like a fool and a nonsense."

"Bon Dyé! My God, is so people like to bad talk eh? What you tell her?"

"What you think I can say? It don't matter. I didn't answer. I just shake my head as if to say all dat is stupidness. But I make up my mind to go away for a little while, let things cool down a little. I going country by my sister. That's what I come to tell you."

"When you going?"

"Saturday. Day after tomorrow. I taking the early bus. Is a long drive. But I will come tomorrow morning as usual to say goodbye."

The next morning he came through the yard and she opened the kitchen door to let him in. She closed the door as he entered, reached for his hand and led him directly into her room. Neither said a word. They clung to each other and Albertine moved with a vigour she had not shown in the year they had been together. Alphonse was gasping intermittently, but she was carried away by a surge of passion which was more intense because he would be leaving. Over the heavy thud of her heartbeat she heard Alphonse call "Bertina!" in a muffled voice, then she felt his dead weight against her body.

Albertine was nowhere to be found later when a small group gathered in front of her house. Marie, Alphonse's wife, had entered and after an hour or so a hearse arrived and two attendants went in and emerged shortly afterwards carrying a body covered in a sheet on a stretcher. Marie followed them holding a pair of sneakers in her hands. Her mouth was set in a thin line as she watched them put the body into the hearse. As the hearse drove away she turned, walked down the sidewalk, and entered her house a few doors away. On the day after the funeral Albertine was seen approaching her house in the opposite direction from Alphonse's house and she was gesticulating as though in conversation, but there was no one with her. There were rumours that she had fled to the country, that she had locked herself in an outhouse in her yard, but no one knew for sure where she had gone the morning Alphonse spilled his dying love over her. Now she always approached her house via a roundabout route, so she avoided walking in front of Alphonse's house. It was clear that she had changed since the events of that morning.

IV

Albertine slowly raised her head. A shaft of sunlight fell on the ribbons that had bound the letters from Cyril. The smell of smoke from the burned letters hung in the kitchen. She wiped her eyes and picked up the ribbons. It finish now, Cyril. I don't have the letters and I don't have to listen to you. You do what you do and it finish. She tilted her head to one side. All she heard was the wind whistling through the wooden louvres of the window. She smiled, got up, shut the louvres, picked up the ribbons and threw them into the garbage. She picked up the flask from the table, shook it and put it back down. Empty. But I okay for now. She turned off the kitchen light, looked around and smiled. Is just like when Alphonse use to come. As she turned to make her way to her room she stopped and tilted her head towards the kitchen door. Is who that so early this morning? She went to the door, opened it and held out her hand. She closed the door, a broad smile on her face. Is really you? Come in, my dear.

THREE POEMS

Zahra Gordon

ANCESTRY

Picture Rhoda Agatha Foncette,
née Reid and known as such
— a buxom beauty stationed in the nave
like an ebony tower; eight properly
dressed children trailing behind her.

Picture Rhoda making the sign of the cross;
middle and index fingers pressing firmly
against forehead, silk-blend bodice, shoulders;
knees bent to curtsey acknowledging the only man
who could make her bow.

Picture Rhoda one hour late for church;

making her way to the front-most pew;

each step closer to the altar a building block

in the boldface legacy I inherited.

Licks Like Rain

I

She should've been familiar with the types of hands that beat;
recognised the firm grip he kept on a glass while drinking;
the bitten bottom lip and pregnant fist that shadowed simple
    mistakes.
When you find yourself useless, tender body limp at the root of a
    mango tree,
from a father-inflicted 2x4 lash, only rainfall to rinse the blood on
    your forehead,
you become familiar with those types of hands — hands with long,
    slender fingers

acting on behalf of unfulfilled dreams.

You come to understand that disrespect is a one-way street travelled
    only by women.

She should've been familiar, but she didn't read between the lines
    of his love letters,
didn't hear the licks in his raging drum solos.

II

When the licks and the marriage failed, he turned to stalking.
She found reprieve in America with restraining orders,
thanked God for the partial anonymity of New York.

III

When she remarried, she wore a sky-blue, spaghetti-strap dress,
    which shimmered only lightly.
No white. No veil. No lace. No doting bridesmaids, cathedral of
    flowers or army band like the first wedding.   Before she
    said I do, she examined her second husband's hands one final
    time.

GRAVEYARD

I hope there are poems waiting for me at my father's grave.

I've never seen his tombstone so I don't know what epitaph is
    engraved on it, what inspiration is etched into the font used to
    write his name, sunrise, sunset.

All I remember is a mound of dirt swallowing a closed casket; my
    aunt pushing white roses into my hand saying, Look, put
    some flowers for your father;

and that evening months later when Ms St Cyr took me back to the
    cemetery after pan practice,
and we drove around aimlessly until it was too dark for us to find
    him, too late for me to leave another bouquet or a message
    because this was no All Saints' or All Souls' night with the
    neighbours to keep you company while you placed cheap,
    white tapers around your loved ones' graves and sang hymns to
    praise
the dead;

this was not longtime when I was a child more concerned with
    making candle balls and scraping stiff wax from my fingers

before bedtime than saying prayers for great-grandparents I
knew only through stories;

this was not those afternoons on November 1st and 2nd when I
anticipated with friends staying up late, being outside at
midnight;

this was not November 3rd when I put those candle balls in my
book-bag hoping mine was the largest;

this was definitely not my twenties when it had rum and rhythm
section and the good Christians rested their floral
arrangements early o'clock and hurried to light their candles
before the limers invited souls to fete

because Mt Lebanon Cemetery is a gated community; it doesn't stay
open all night for you to pay tribute, reminisce, or dance.

Every grave has a mailing address, and I can't remember where my
father lives.

MAN CRUSH — TAKE FIVE

Philip Nanton

TAKE ONE

He-roooes! Talking 'bout he-roes
he-roes, he-roes.
He-roooes! Talking 'bout he-roes
he-roes, he-roes *

TAKE TWO

You could call it a man crush. It started a long time ago. My cousin
represented a certain kind of glamour that has never faded though
our paths cross only occasionally. Some eight years older than me,
he had the gift of a ready smile, an easygoing nonchalance that
accompanied a talent for playing the guitar. I remember plucking the
metal strings and feeling how sharp and awkward they were under

* W. Farrell (2011) "Talking 'Bout Heroes" in *Bustin' the Blues: A Collection of Poems:*
Caribbean Chapters Publishing, Barbados, p 138

my fingers. The working of both hands independently to make the right note still seems a kind of magic, one that I never mastered. So there was awe and admiration and, yes, perhaps some envy. Wanting the skill but not wanting it enough to put in the time to acquire it.

Derek Walcott put his finger on an important Caribbean characteristic, one that my cousin acquired naturally. For us, performance is essential, he observed. We don't do small and apologetic. We make noise, draw attention to ourselves. And when that noise is sweet . . . Because of his sweet noise, my cousin's life seemed more dramatic than mine. His father had walked out when he was young. Then the family moved from St Vincent to Grenada and on to Trinidad. Toughened through a social falling from small island grace, they had learned to survive. As a young teenager, he was leading his first band in Grenada: by the age of sixteen he was living in a boarding house in Port of Spain. In his twenties he was playing with three different kinds of bands in the Trinidad music scene. If you have a talent for music, then Port of Spain is a good place to learn to survive and even thrive.

When my cousin was forming his first band I was busy avoiding licks in school, visiting boring aunts who spoke in strange accents, doing homework and attending confirmation classes. I was encouraged to be seen and not heard. But then how do you tell when you are grown up? Long pants, job, froth in your pee? Perhaps it involves even bigger events. After many years I met again recently a man from Montserrat who used to stand in line next to me on most Sunday mornings in our Bridgetown suburb when we went to buy our coconut water. I told him I was building a house. He replied, "that is when you become a man in these parts." Or perhaps it is when your hero becomes human and you see him differently, with cooler eyes. But the scales do not have to fall all at once. This is how they fell.

There was some common ground. For some time, neither of us

really knew our fathers. His went off to war soon after my cousin was born; mine was of the Victorian type, formal and austere. We both did our time in England, his was much shorter and by choice. I was sent as a teenager and stayed much longer. Whether the stay was long or short we both had to make a choice, either to stay there or return to the Caribbean. His shorter stay only made him more glamorous, as he was soon leading a band in London — getting gigs in dingy town halls, at student balls and eventually on TV. After what seemed to me like a few short years he went back to Trinidad. I stayed in England to beat the books and fight the cold, becoming a cultural analyst with a university job. Then, out of the blue, one day there was a signed copy of his first vinyl LP made in Trinidad. There were to be five in all, among many other musical achievements. By then he had his own business, house, wife and children. The music could not be given up but it just did not pay if you had a family to support.

Back in the Caribbean for a while, I visited him in Trinidad. It was my first Carnival there and he was my guide to many fetes. I knew what it was all about, yet I did not know it. We played pretty mass with Edmond Hart's band. I remember a kaleidoscope of Monday colour, dust and a goatskin full of rum. That Monday our band section diverted from the route through a hotel swimming pool. On Carnival Tuesday, in shrunken costumes, we went through the pool again. But it had been emptied, except for the deep end. When I climbed out the water was a glittering black mass, marinated with mascara and face paint.

TIME PASSED

To write all this requires some distance. So when does distance start? Perhaps it starts when you learn to recognise a word like "charisma."

When you start to ask, what does this kind of Caribbean music do? Who is the audience?

TAKE THREE

For Gordon Rohlehr, Caribbean artists characteristically reflect the nostalgia of an urban audience for a perceived ideal of community and countryside. In his collection of essays *A Scuffling of Islands: The Dream and Reality of Caribbean Unity in Poetry and Song* he argues that "fragments of the dream remain lodged in the brain of the region's artists, academics and technocrats, and it is with these fragments that the region's singers will work."

TAKE FOUR

Short, dark complexion, a mass of wavy black hair making his age indeterminate. On stage he sits behind the microphone, wearing a bright maroon shirt. His trousers are cream, his shoes shine. A light-colored Godin guitar rests across his knee, one arm gently cradling the instrument. A broad smile lights his eyes and mouth. It is the smile of an experienced showman, confident in his ability to command his audience. Alone on stage he will begin with a deep chuckle, followed by: "You know . . ." or "You ever hear 'bout . . . ?" The story he tells may be his version of the history of steelpan music, the differences between styles of parang or quatro playing, or the story of the indigenous cocrico bird. The Trinidad lilt of his speaking voice hovers a few octaves below his singing voice. He uses this voice, the chuckle, and his gentle authority to charm his audience into following him wherever he chooses to go. In his audience the women can easily afford a new outfit for the occasion. The men, fewer in number, are happy to put their professional cares behind them for a few hours. His confidence and style convince them that they are in safe hands. The artistry offers them a reassurance that they eagerly receive.

TAKE FIVE

In this incarnation, my cousin's story of the history of pan is a seamless presentation with no breaks, false starts, or wrong turnings, recalling patterns of early music-making, reviving famous names in the history of pan, and performing a number of tunes. The combination of story, song, and guitar-playing encapsulates one instrument's homage to another. The storytelling presents an uncomplicated line of development, from bamboo to dustbins and hubcaps to modern pan. The audience's nostalgia is kindled through popular song and gentle humour, reminding them of their history in an unbroken arc that appeals to Trinidadian nationalism. It is an optimistic story, which ultimately says ,"look how far we have developed"; a message removed from Caribbean popular music's lament — having been cheated by history, by women, and by the system. His storytelling and lyrics call down a folk-based benediction on the Caribbean, similar in spirit to David Rudder's soca incantations.

It was around music that we met and parted and met again. I came to realise that forty years away had made me an outsider, and so there was just one less adoring fan in the audience.

FOUR POEMS

Lynn Sweeting

After the Vote

What do you do after the vote?
Cry, die, come back again,
it can't be helped.

You don't ask for resurrection,
it is forced upon you
like a sexist constitution,
like a backward people.

You don't want to go outside,
but you need things,

you don't want to make eye contact
with your people, your sisters,
but school's out and you have to
pick up your daughter,
cry, die, come back again,
you don't know why
you keep on moving
though you've died.

You do something mundane
to calm yourself down,
leaf through your manuscript,
count the pages,
put unpublished poems
in a neat pile,
check deadline dates,
count the days you have left
to get an entry in the mail,
cry, die, come back again,
it can't be avoided,
you don't get a vote this time.

The sun will carry you
into the new day whether
you want to go or not,

compel you to keep your head up,
to smile at people
as if you didn't suspect them,
coerce you to write poems
from the point of view
of the hopeful one
when all hope is lost,

to cry, die, come back again,
and again, and again,
after the vote you'll keep on living
even if it kills you.

Getting Out of Poetry's Way

What if I threw open the door of my heart
and set all my wild angels free?
They wouldn't care one bit what race or nation
produced, embraced, or rejected me,
they'd circle dance around me the same
as for the one who saw her face in the mirror,
the one who knew her own authentic name.

What if I told you I am not grateful
for injuries that bled these words upon the page?
The wild Madeira is not aghast to know
that like Jean Rhys, if I'd had the choice
I'd have chosen the silence of the unwound
over writing in this journal every time,
the availability of water over the longing for wine.

The grave and the birthing bed are not
poles apart from one another,
the heron drinking at the cold pool knows
they are one and the same place where
only the light changes as Earth spins round,
that what lies beneath the feet of the midwife
and the gravedigger is the same sacred ground.

The wind is cold for March but I love it anyway,
my coffee is bitter more often than it is good,
but I'm amazed how I keep on making it anyway,
the blooming hibiscus and the dead branch
are children of the same bush and equally loved.
Having no need of my words the dove flies west
into the sun that dies so tomorrow can live.

LANGUAGE OF THE GARDEN

Hibiscus
doesn't cry
for perfume
she wasn't given,
she's too busy being
redder than
a woman's blood,
big as a moon
rising full over a field
of creeping crabgrass.

Hummingbird
never grieves
the big bad bird
she might have been,
or begrudges the hawk
his lizard lunch,
she concerns herself
with her nest
of bejewelled babies,
with pollinating heliconias.

Poet,

on the island

she never left,

and never will leave,

croton-crowned,

sun-browned,

doesn't wish for leaving

when she sits down to write,

but for the language of the garden

that has grown her.

Advice From the Boa

Listen, you don't need to be afraid

when you're waiting for the next poem to come along,

not even when the last one was a month ago,

and your belly is hungering,

the moment of its arrival is always at hand.

Never weep for the old skin when it splits open,

let it fall away and leave it lovingly as an offering,

the woman you were is your attending spirit,

the woman you are is the one she birthed,

the shining new skin you wear is her best gift to you.

Find a tree among other trees and there make your home,

from canopy to roots you will always find refuge,

take sun on the eastern branches in the mornings,

keep closer to Earth in the black of the long night eyes open,

watch for what sustains you throwing shadows on the moon.

GOAL

Barbara Jenkins

Indira sizes up the bald little man standing at the doorway of De Rightest Place. Kitted out in a gold turtleneck long-sleeved jumper and black shorts with gold side stripes, his sparkly teeth flashing in a wide smile, he hops from one gold football boot to the other, the gold whistle suspended by a black ribbon around his neck swinging from side to side in synchronicity with his skipping dance. His gilt bonhomie could not be more at odds with Indira's mood. The post lady, her first caller this morning, set it at black and blue when she handed over that stash of envelopes.

The visitor introduces himself by showing her a red card.

The Reverend Pastor U.R. Sukker
God Ordains Alternative Lifestyles.
www.ministryofGOAL.com

She flicks the card with her fingers.
You're this person? The pastor?
He takes the gold whistle to his lips and emits a shrill blast.

Goal!

You sure you in the right place? This is a pub.

Another ear-splitting blast, and again, Goal!

As the whistle falls from his lips, Indira reaches out and grasps it firmly.

What can I do for you?

Perchance I could have the honour of conference with the lady identified on the façade of this property as the proprietress and licensee, one Indira Gabriel?

She releases the whistle.

That's me.

Charmed, I'm sure. If it behoves you to bestow the pleasure of your company on your humble servant?

I already have a religion and I don't want to change it.

Ha-ha. No-no. Your conclusions are not appropriate to the situation here present. No-no-no. Not at all. Ha-ha. May I have the temerity to offer a little business proposition that will bestow mutual satisfaction and benefit to the two parties here present, that is to say — me, party of the first part and thee, party of the second part?

On two conditions. First. Do not blow that whistle again. Second. Hi-falutin' English is not my first language. So, speak simply. Understand?

He looks a little crestfallen, but he nods. Indira continues.

Drink? We have a large stock of non-alcoholic beverages.

And alcoholic ones?

What would you like?

Sitting opposite him, Indira allows him to sip his foaming Carib in silence for just a scant minute. She pushes aside her own untouched Cuba libre and drums a quick staccato on the table.

What's up?

It is my urgent and overwhelming desire to locate my esteemed edifice of worship on your salubrious hereditament.

Indira raises her arm yellow-card style.

Ahem. I want to set up my church here.

Indira chides herself for her slip-up. How naïve of her not to interpret the blatant clues. A madman! She'd bet her bottom dollar he's an escapee from the asylum. Glancing around under her lashes, she checks her exit route. The table would bar his way as she makes a dash for the door. She'll throw a metal chair at him when he lunges for her. In the meantime, she will go along with him. Who knows what he might do if she lets on she's suspicious.

Uh-huh. Here. Okay. Okay. Here. When?

Saturday.

Def-in-it-ely cuckoo. Every weekend this place is crammed with sinners who have no desire for repentance. And I, Indira, have no interest in them repenting either. There's the lucrative wages of sin to consider. But what to do? Safer to keep on humouring him, until.

Here is very busy on weekends, you know, she says gently, as if explaining to a foreigner with limited knowledge of the culture.

Not inside. No-no. Not here. Ha-ha-ha. It's your backyard I'm interested in. I already took a walk around. It's De Rightest Place for a tent. Ha-ha-ha.

And?

The Ministry of God Ordains Alternative Lifestyles is planning a nine-night crusade. My branch preaches Sport as a Way to Salvation.

Your branch?

Yes. Mine. The Salvation Tree has many branches. Its roots can be traced to the original Tree of Knowledge.

Indira nods absently, her eyes darting from the pastor to the door, door to pastor, and back again. He's on a roll, oblivious to her distractedness.

Other branches preach different things. For example, there's Chutney Dancing as a Way to Salvation, Highway Construction as a Way to Salvation, Trawling, Quarrying, even Street-vending. Gay and Trans Life too. We cater for the full spectrum of Trinbagonian social, cultural, economic, and political activity. We're an all-inclusive church.

Not many of those around. So?

You've been selected. What say you?

We haven't talked transfer fee.

He shoots her an admiring glance. Her stare freezes his hand as it reaches for the whistle. He flashes his toothy smile and offers her a fee so attractive that she is tempted to grab his whistle and blow it herself. Exercising restraint, she simply returns his smile. Fifty percent up front; the remainder at the end. She's already calculating how the money will be spent. Which holes plugged, to which channels some diverted. They talk some more about dates and times. As she sees him out, she tells him that she'll finalise the following day. She must make the necessary arrangements with her teammates.

A pastor as an answer to a prayer? Indira is too well honed by hard life to believe it's more than coincidence. But, his stepping into De Rightest Place with his proposition on the very same morning as the credit card statement and the warning letter from Winning Streak Gaming Club's lawyer is a gift horse whose teeth she isn't going to examine. This could be her best chance to pay off that debt, pay bills, and get back on track.

When the pub closes for siesta, Indira calls a meeting with Bostic and Fritzie.

Two matters have come up that we must talk about. First of all, the post brought a couple hefty bills. Water and Electricity. Both threatening disconnection. Secondly, we have an offer from a pastor to rent the yard for a crusade starting Saturday.

Wait-wait-wait, says Fritzie. Is Saturday you saying?

Yes. From Saturday every night for nine nights, five to nine pm.

Bostic intervenes.

So what about the regular trade?

Everything will go on as usual.

He leans back in his chair and waves a dismissive hand towards Indira.

Chuts. You can't be serious. Bar and church can't mix.

C'mon, Bostic. Go brave for a change.

Bostic sits bolt upright.

Brave or reckless? Think about it. Is okay with the neighbours that you turn your downstairs into a bar because here is like they home from home. But tent church? That does draw big, big crowd. It bound to have people coming in from outside. Strangers. You ever check and see how much cars does be park up here any day and night of the week? If it had, say, twenty, or even only ten more cars park up for four, five hours, there could be trouble.

It's only for nine nights. People will adjust.

We hardly get over the disaster of the all-inclusive Carnival fete and you want to take on a next scheme?

You can hardly blame me for that. How could I have predicted that Councillor Ramluck would roll up with his drunken partners and pick a fight with Councillor Morris and his drunken crew?

Is not you self who give them councillors complimentary tickets? Giving complimentary to big shot is like open season. Them so don't go nowhere without a whole posse of hangers-on to laugh at they lame jokes and big them up.

That wouldn't have been a bad thing if they'd only conducted themselves in a more responsible manner.

Indira, when last you hear bout never-see-come-see politician behaving responsible, eh? What it was that former Prime Minister did say one time? "Politics have its own morality."

I can't see what that has to do with the matter in hand.

Plenty, Indira, plenty. Is different strokes for different folks. You don't see how when fight break out small fry does pick up empty bottle to pelt, but big sawatee only pelting full bottle of booze? I never see so much a Grey Goose, Johnny Blue, Jack Daniels flying through the air. Jeezanages! Must be about twenty cases before the police reach. Police self was staggering around, drunk from just breathing in the fumes. You remember that, Fritzie? And, after they done mashup the place, them sons-a-bitches councillors wouldn't pay Indira for the bottles of alcohol they waste when she send the bill. You remember how they say the ticket say unlimited premium bar? Eh?

Fritzie will not be drawn. She goes back to the first issue.

What about the utility bills? The crusade money can cover that, Indira?

For the second time that day, Indira smiles. Yes. It can. Plus we will make a big pot of corn soup to sell after the service. Churchgoers will be hungry after the exertion of testifying.

Who making soup?

You and me, Fritzie. Just like we do for the lunch trade. It's only to make a second batch.

On her way home Fritzie is pondering. What's the matter with Indira these days? Falling for any and every bogus scheme anybody throw at her. Between that and the new craze for casino, casino, every chance she could get away from the bar, she acting well strange. What happening with her? And is all a we to ketch. More work, work, work. Like we don't have a life.

The first of the nine nights goes down well. A good size church crowd, sales brisk in bar and corn soup. Except for two things. One, Bostic and Fritzie are worn ragged. And two, the noise of the sound system blasting the sermon, the testifying, the hymns, setting the neighbours' nerves on edge.

Second night, Sunday, just as good for bar and soup, just as tiring for the team. And so it goes on till Thursday evening.

It so happens that Cynthia is hosting a family christening party on Thursday, at her home, just down the road from De Rightest Place. Car with macomere come, nowhere to park, car with compere come, nowhere to park, car with baby, baby's mother, baby's father, baby's mother's mother and father come and nowhere to park. The street full up both sides with congregation cars. Traffic squeezing past in both directions. Cars circling block after block until they find a space here and there way out by the Savannah, and people have to walk blocks to reach a little "ice cream and cake" party, a little "drink a rum on the baby's head" party. And, the final nail in the coffin, when Cynthia's guests put on music to really party, a little *raise yuh han', wine down low,* it's getting drowned out by *washed in the blood of the lamb* coming from the tent church in Indira's yard.

By four o'clock on Friday, the swelling number of converts to GOAL Ministries take up all the street parking. Residents have to abandon their precious vehicles that they're still paying for, far, far away, at the mercy of opportunistic car thieves, and they have to hoof it home. Bostic and Fritzie are already frazzled by the relentless demand from the pious for soup and refreshment.

Friday turns to Saturday, the eighth night of the crusade. Residents launch a car parking offensive. Off work for the weekend, they occupy the streets with their cars from early. They call family and friends to park in the remaining spaces. Late afternoon rolls by. A churchgoer pulls up, her car partly blocking the entrance to a driveway. Leaving the engine running to keep the air-conditioning on, she lifts out her one-year-old, runs into the tent with him for his granny to look after, so she could go back to her car, drive until she finds a real space, park up, and then walk back with the six-year-old who is sleeping in the car. When she hustles back to where she left the car, it and her little girl are gone.

She dials the emergency number to report her missing car with child inside. Five long minutes pass as she listens to a recorded voice giving options, presses numbers, receives more recorded instructions and finally hears, all our agents are busy now. Please stay on the line. Your call is important to us. She runs back to the tent church. It is now packed full and late arrivals are standing about in little groups in the yard. She approaches one cluster and tells them what has happened. Someone offers to drive her to the nearest police station and its presiding sergeant.

Where you say your vehicle was park? Madam, you come to the wrong station. That vehicle was park outside this jurisdiction. You have to make your report at the station on the Circular Road.

At the Circular Road Station, bench loads of people are waiting to report accidents, break-ins, shootings and other everyday difficulties of life to a lone officer, hunched over pages of tortured longhand. One hour pass before it's her turn and the officer says that the missing *car* can be reported there. The missing *child* has to be reported elsewhere, in the jurisdiction of the child's residence.

In the meantime, rippling from one group of churchgoers outside the tent to the next, a wave of whispering flows inside, surging through the congregation as a murmuring mumbling, a lowering and nodding of heads, a shuffling of feet, a standing up, walking about, dashing around as the word spreads. They teef a lady car. A little girl get kidnap. The flock streams out, making enquiries on the street. They discover that a resident phoned Traffic Branch to haul away offending vehicles, that cars were towed, that it's a possibility that the child and car are lodged in one of the five or so car pounds in the city. Teams of churchgoers fan out in search, and the vehicle is located in the yard of the Police Ghetto Observation Post at the eastern edge of the city.

The finders have to wait for the mother to come. When she gets there the police do not let her take her child or her car. They send her home to fetch the child's birth certificate and the certificate of ownership for the car, to prove that both belong to her. They check her driver's permit and the car insurance certificate. She pays the five hundred dollar fine for illegal parking and as she turns to leave with her little girl, the policeman tells her, this time I letting you off with a warning. Allyuh woman too damn careless. You lucky I not laying a charge on you for child neglect.

Back at the GOAL tent church, the Reverend Pastor Sukker's shrill whistle summons the residue of the congregation not involved in the car search to come inside, come forward, up, up, to the front, to stay on the pitch, stay in the game. It will not be always like this, he says. No where to park. No where to sit. This is just the start. Your own clubhouse awaits you. Imagine such a place, he says. You will not need that fan you are waving, sister; no need to mop your brow, brother; the clubhouse, your clubhouse, will be fully air-conditioned. Our sister who had her car wrecked will drive into our secure car park. And you, brothers and sisters, who came in from the sidelines to sit on these plastic chairs, picture your new stands — row upon row of comfortable seating, padded, backrest, armrest, a veritable throne for each and every one. Fellow teammates at the back. Are you straining your eyes to see? Stretching your ears to hear? No more. No more. You will lift up thine eyes to wide screen plasma TVs hung all along the walls. Can we do it? Yes we can! Yes we can! But only if we all have the will to win. Only if we pull together, work as a team, keep our eyes on the ball. Send your contribution flying into the GOAL net.

Sunday dawns bright and hopeful. The priest at the more established religious institution, the one whose congregation is made up of the residents of this settled community, preaches his interpretation of the Sermon on the Mount. The reminder from the pulpit of loaves and fishes, generosity, sharing, brotherly love, do-unto-others, that sort of thing, strikes a guilty chord in the hearts of the neighbours. They file out of the church in near silence. Nobody talks about the incident of the evening before, but all who have off-street parking drive their vehicles into their carports.

It's the last night of the nine nights crusade at the GOAL Ministries. It's four on that dozy Sunday afternoon. Pastor U.R. Sukker is standing on the pavement glancing up and down the street. The street is as empty as the national treasury after a five-year unrestricted raid by a ruling party. A mere sprinkling of neighbours' cars; no neighbours' family and friends' cars; no congregation cars either. He pulls up a gold sleeve and checks his watch over and over again, as if it's an itch that needs constant scratching. At five, he goes into the tent and stands at the pulpit. He looks around. From overflowing on Saturday at the start of service to now, the tent is almost drained of congregation. He is not so misguided as to count as lasting converts Cecil, Boyee, Feroze, and Anil, who've dropped in out of Sunday afternoon ennui. What went wrong? He ponders. It wasn't his sermons. He brings to mind the resounding singing, the ardent testifying, the thunderous clapping with which his performance was greeted every night for the past eight nights. He knows he scored hat trick after hat trick. And now this?

Alas, what was to have been a crescendo of salvation and a torrent of tithes on the big night, the Finals of the Deliverance Cup, as it were, is reduced to a feeble affirmation from that handful of faithful who live in easy walking distance of the tent, and a mere trickle of offerings into the GOAL net. Pastor can't meet the second payment. The goalposts shifted, he explains to Indira. Indira has to admit to herself that she's scored an own goal this time. But all is not lost. She has her own goals to consider. Forward ever. Backward never.

Next morning, Indira, Bostic, and Fritzie meet for a post mortem. From a huge pot of corn soup on the bar counter, the stench of fermenting grain wafts to where the three are sitting. Indira throws a glance at Bostic, slouched down, eyes closed, as she clears away from the table a clutter of empty beer bottles. Okay, okay, she says. So, it didn't quite work out as planned. Bostic briefly flickers open one eyelid, lizard-style, and shifts in his chair. Fritzie looks studiously at her nails and begins to scrape off flaking nail polish with a thumbnail. Neither looks at Indira. You know what went wrong? Indira continues. Not enough parking. This is a busy little street at the best of times. Here's what. I'll get the backyard paved and mark off some parking spots. We can charge people to park their cars. What do you think?

FOUR POEMS

Monica Minott

HORSE-HEAD

The line picked up speed like Horse-head,
a name deserved, "Him a de real sin-ting." He learn
to bow and scrape, turn sample into simple. Show
too much, too soon; like how white people jump
before the reggae-beat drop, before the rhythm
soak, is like a secret society move, most of us
don't understand de-signs, but know to keep out,
yet they feel slighted when we laugh.
Not everything you know you show.
Horse-head never learn this lesson,

have no reserve when hungry tek him;
him sell birthright for next to nothing.
Foreigner put up fence, "Keep Out."
Horse-head never learn fe play fool
 fi catch wise, him head big, carrying
only fear; and good for nothing.

A Beautiful Corpse

Jean-Michel Basquiat, 1961–1988

The art dealers lined up.
Yes, he was indeed beautiful. Yet
they left before we buried his body.
His going had no code, body laid out.
It was time for the counting:
the rains came.

I got a hole in my soul
I heard Jean-Michel say, a hole
so large, only death can
fill it. I got a hole in my
pocket, I heard the answer
just one more painting
before you go!

Rundown

Mama took the kitchen cloth
and dabbed her eyes hoping
none of her children would see.
Peeling the yellow yam,
Mama know when starch dry
it go well with the rundown
simmering in the dutch pot.

Outside the kitchen window
boys play marbles, girls pretend
to be Mamas on tippy toes.
A smile opens her memory.
She once played dress-up, swishing
bony hips down an imaginary catwalk,
and where did it get her? Over a stove
watching the persistent tide pull back
much of what it had promised;

Mama watch cracks in earth
swallow jazz shoes, as brush strokes
fade, while rotting husks of coconut
drift out to sea, each husk a log entry
recording a would-be landfall.

She shut her eyes tight, desperate
to stem the flow of tears gathering;
kneading dumplings into compliance
peeling and trimming knots in yam
dicing potatoes, grating coconuts
weeping again into our next meal.

"THE SEA WILL CLAIM US ALL"

For Grandfather Cecil Campbell

Stones tossed from another shore,
we rewrite our language into creole.
Who hears tragedy in oceans, in shells,
in tongues, when our feet become fins?

We leave exposed cracks in contours
of a continent, in the eclipse of Africa,
colour-stains rain from wounded reefs;
cure-all salt of the earth travelling free

like tragedy, we get here. I am but one
fragment, washed-up on an eastern shore.
Yet you sail west to find something of me;
of Columbus's "horned monsters," I dream

a kinked soul, epicentre of an ocean's
quarrels. It's no longer about Odysseus
and shipwrecks, he has done his time
on earth. Earth guts and drowns old fish

and sailors. I mourn a grandfather.
I follow a moving finger's trajectory,
a rising of mad blackbirds; my brother
flashes crazy-mean locks at the sky.

I'm with him in a landlocked cove,
in the haze of smoke from a man-spliff
he pulls against the old secret of the
sea's selection, man overboard — his name

Cecil. The humming of the ocean makes
one sick, the drag of water heavy on his
legs, Cecil finds release in the grip of tides
like a woman's leg locked in contradiction

to her heart. Blood stains mark sea stones.
We travel in silence, migrating sun-bodies,
skeletal minds; surfs hesitate to bring the
news, "man lost at sea."

G&TS AND RITA BLOODY MARLEY

Lisa Allen-Agostini

"Rita Bloody Marley."

She poured herself an inch of gin, waved a bottle of tonic water in its general vicinity, and squeezed a lime in the glass before plopping a couple of ice cubes into the viscous mixture. Her face looked the way I'd expected it to when she tasted it, but she seemed to find it satisfactory and took another sip.

"They all had this idea in their head that they could get away with it. Rita bloody Marley."

Another sip. By now I could smell the raw, bitter gin, the sour lime. It made my mouth water, but she drank it down and made herself another. Well, Tante Alice was getting her vitamin C in for sure, I thought. Pity about her liver.

You'd never guess, looking at her, that this woman drank as much as she did. She was one of those delicate-looking, light-skinned, middle-class black Caribbean women of a certain age, one who wore tidy dresses and had most of her own teeth, who pronounced her tee-aiches: always "that," never "dat," always "there," never "dere." Even now, when I was the only visitor she had, she was pristine and polite, as if ready to drop everything and head to a tea party at a moment's notice.

I only came to do the washing, to tidy up her husband, and to prepare a week's worth of food in five hours, freeze it, and leave. She paid me minimum wage, which didn't do much to offset my costs as a full-time university student. It was all she could afford; she was my aunt and I would have done it for free, but she wouldn't hear of it. My real payment came in the stories she told as she followed me around the house, sipping her gin and tonics and growing increasingly jolly or bitter, depending on the day, depending on her mood and his.

When Uncle Peter was good, she was horrid. She hated his good days. They made her bitter and the nearest thing to rude you'd ever get from her: a kind of snide, sarcastic flippancy in which everyone became "Darling," said in a malicious drawl that made one feel an inch tall. As in, "Darling, if you don't cook the rice better than that I'm afraid I'll lose my remaining teeth. Please don't sacrifice dentistry in the cause of quick cooking, darling."

When he had bad days, she was cheerful and whimsical. "Oh, don't bother about the rice. I'll cook it myself when I'm ready to eat." Which was a lie, of course. She wouldn't turn on the stove; it was microwaved food or nothing for her these days, hence my weekly pilgrimage to her home to stock the fridge and freezer.

And today, while I steamed broccoli and carrots, boiled whole wheat pasta and sautéed chicken breasts in heart-healthy olive oil, she puttered around in my wake describing cocktail parties that had taken place forty years before.

"Could you imagine, darling?" she drawled. "This insignificant little man flirting with that creature right in front of me. And had the gall. The absolute. Gall. To compare her to me. As if, darling. Some kind of guttersnipe from deepest South. You couldn't understand a word she said. Magnificent hair, though. Amazing what blue soap and coconut oil can do."

And another sip of gin later, she was reeling into another story about her unfaithful, ungrateful husband.

"When he was sleeping with the maid — Malarial Maria, do you remember her? — he would think he was so clever. Always giving her extra money for 'medicine.' As though I couldn't count. Silly bastard. 'But darling,' I'd say, 'why are we giving Maria another loan? Surely her malaria is better now.' And he'd brush me aside and put another blue note into her pay packet. Which was really my pin money, you understand. A hundred dollars was so much money back then. He was taking money out of my pocket to give to his whore. And, darling, she was such a terrible cook. Couldn't even make pelau." She shuddered delicately.

"I've never seen you eat pelau," I reminded her.

"Darling, but I love pelau! Such a perfect mélange of rice, coconut milk, pigeon peas, caramel colouring, meat, and veg! It's wonderful!"

"I didn't know you felt that strongly about it. And here am I cooking steamed chicken breasts and broccoli." I smiled ironically; the food was doctor's orders. Tante Alice had a list of meal options taped to the fridge, and most of the items on the list were steamed or roasted, high-fibre and low-fat. I would bet that anything cooked in coconut milk was absolutely out of the question.

"But, darling, that's his menu. I can eat whatever I want! Don't tell me you've made me suffer all this time for no reason, darling." Perfectly manicured pink nails fluffed her white hair. She had told me she went to bed in curlers every night but still wore a satin negligee to bed. She slept alone in a bedroom adjoining his; had done so since I started helping her out four years before, when he had the stroke. Her bedroom was immaculate, with ruffled sheets she changed herself, and different sets of lacy curtains I hung for her four times a year.

Back when I first started coming every week she hid the gin in a pitcher in the fridge. Now she no longer bothered to pretend that her afternoon drinks were anything but gin-soaked lime juice.

Melting ice tinkled in her crystal highball glass as she shook it to mix the drink. "Darling, you have to make me some pelau. This instant. Do it at once." She propped herself up on the stool next to the kitchen island to make sure I did.

"But we don't have any coconut," I protested. It was true. "You can't make pelau without coconut."

"I've heard it can be done with regular milk."

"Yes, but."

"But?"

"If you're doing it, do it right, my mother always said."

She took a drink and slid off the kitchen stool. "So true, darling. What a clever baby sister I had. Next time you come, bring a coconut."

Tante Alice was perfectly coiffed as usual when I went the following week. Uncle Peter was having a terrible day. His bedroom stank of urine. He glanced at me with glassy eyes as I changed his damp sheets and sprayed Lysol on the plastic mattress cover underneath him. "Are you . . . Maria?" he asked in a halting voice. He sounded like someone struggling to remember not just names, but words themselves.

We both jumped when the front door slammed shut. A breeze, I told myself.

Tante Alice came to the bedroom door, glittering crystal in her hand, and a half smile on her coral lips.

"You'd want Maria to see you like this, Peter? With your limp dick swilling around in pissy diapers? Oh, Peter." Her laughter tinkled like the sound of the ice in her glass.

Crestfallen, Uncle Peter covered his face with a shrivelled hand.

"Oh, buck up, Pete! Your nice young niece will take care of you. She's cooking pelau today!"

He said nothing, but a look of such revulsion crossed his face that I jumped back. His good hand shot out, snakelike, to clutch my wrist. I couldn't read the look in his eyes, I told myself, prising his hand off before changing the sheets and airing out the bedroom.

"Before we were married, my pelau was the best in the country," Tante Alice boasted loudly, following me with my armload of stinking sheets to the laundry room. Her thirty-year-old washer still worked. I think she secretly had a crush on the repairman who came to service it every six months, but she would never admit it.

"Let's just say he keeps my pipes in excellent order," she would joke, winking and sipping her gin. "Working pipes are terribly important to a housewife, you know," she added with an angelic look on her wrinkled face.

The sheets went into a tub of hot water with bleach and detergent. They'd come out smelling like roses and I'd make sure to leave them where she could find them, but I knew that I'd come back the following week to find Uncle Peter in much the same condition as I'd left him. She changed his diapers, fed him, and that was it. She left his false teeth floating in the glass beside his bed; wouldn't even turn on the TV to let him watch the news anymore. She claimed she wasn't strong enough to change his sheets, but we both knew better.

Revenge is best served cold. Cold and damp and smelling like week-old piss.

A whole fryer. I jointed it, then cut each piece until I had a bowl of bony chicken fragments each about an inch cubed. I washed them in lime — "Of course you can, sweet girl! My limes are your limes!" Tante had said cheerfully — and seasoned them in onion, chive, garlic, soy sauce, and thyme. I set the chicken in the fridge to marinate and returned to Uncle Peter's bedroom.

I checked his medication on the bedside table, the baby aspirin and digoxin for his heart, and the thousand other pills and potions his doctor prescribed for his wasted right side and withering left side. He'd lost weight steadily since I'd been working for them, and I didn't doubt he was now willing himself to die. His toothless mouth hung open a little, drooling from the corner, as I dusted and mopped the beige room that had become his only vista. I'd suggested Tante Alice turn the bed so at least he'd see the window, but she'd said, "Darling, don't be silly. What does he need with a view? He was a pilot for forty years, for God's sake. He's had enough spectacular views to last a lifetime." Another sip of gin. "And enough women, too. All those lovely air stewardesses, flying such friendly skies."

She scoffed into her gin.

"Rita bloody Marley."

Creole meat stews in the Caribbean are coloured rich brown with caramelised sugar. You throw meat into oil and bubbling browned sugar, and turn the sizzling pieces in the caramel until each one is coated in this colouring. It's bittersweet, and gives savoury stews a saccharine undertone. Carrots, pumpkin, onions, and tomatoes add to the sweetness, and in a pelau the coconut milk tops it off with a creamy finish. It was practically a national dish. Anybody could cook a pelau, and I didn't fool myself that mine was anything special. But you wouldn't imagine that from Tante Alice's reaction.

I placed a steaming plate in front of her, with the traditional spoonful of coleslaw at the side. Her expression was rapturous. When she had finished a tiny second helping, she set her plate aside and patted her mouth with a paper serviette.

"Whew! What a pelau!" A sip of gin. "You know," she stage-whispered, "he hates pelau. Absolutely hates it. The last time I cooked it he took the whole thing, pot and all, and tossed it out the window, right into the yard. The neighbours..." She blushed. "It was so embarrassing."

But she smiled as she drank, watching me take a dish of that pelau to her husband.

I passed the record player on my way to Uncle Peter's bedroom. I knew he loved music; he had left a pristine record collection in the living room. She never played them, as far as I knew, but she kept them neat and tidy, arranged first by order of name of performer, then name of record. Every now and then I'd find one out on the buffet, but I couldn't imagine Tante Alice playing it. I sometimes wondered what she did with them. Perhaps just looked at the artwork for old times' sake? Swooning at Brook Benton or Nat "King" Cole in their sepia-toned photographs, so debonair and dashing?

Uncle Peter had been as handsome. He still was, in the big wedding photo she had on the buffet. She wore a crown and veil over a white maxi dress, and he wore a tuxedo. The black middle class in wedded bliss, circa 1960.

"It's pelau," I murmured to him. "She said you hate it."

He shook his head, opened his mouth like a grave.

Using the back of a spoon I mashed the rice and peas as best as I could before I shovelled the mess into his mouth. He gummed the food with tears in his eyes.

"Maria," he said again.

I shook my head. "Not Maria," I reminded him. "Abby. You used to dance with me on your feet when I was a baby. Gina's little girl."

"Ahhhh . . ."

"Abby."

"Ah. Bee."

"Yes. Abby."

His moist eyes flashed to the bedside table.

"Water."

He dribbled it down his dirty pyjama top, glanced at the cluttered bedside table again.

"Abby," he said. "Kill."

"What?" I thought he'd said he was ill. Or perhaps I wanted to think that.

Withering or not, the hand that sought to grip my wrist was hard as steel.

I could hear Tante Alice humming happily in the living room.

I bathed him. Tante Alice watched, sipping the G&T as she leaned on the bathroom door. Even when I struggled with his slippery dead weight in the half-full marble tub, she didn't budge to lend a hand. Eventually I flopped him back on the bed; he was as clean now as I was sweaty. He closed his eyes as I put him in fresh diapers, but that steel grip lingered in my memory.

Back in the kitchen, I parcelled out pelau for Tante Alice, but planned to boil yams, dasheen, and cassava for Uncle Peter. He would have that all week, with steamed vegetables and minced beef. Boring, but at least it wasn't pelau. Tante Alice saw me taking the root vegetables out of the fridge.

"Darling," she snapped, "whatever are you doing?"

"I just thought —"

"Darling, nobody needs you to think. Next time, ask before you think. I don't pay you to waste my food, you know. I will feed him the pelau."

I bit my tongue.

While folding the clean sheets, I heard her small, stealthy footsteps behind me. I didn't turn around, even when she shook the ice in her glass. The tinkle of the ice against the crystal was as sharp as a cleared throat. She started talking to my back.

"He beat me, you know. He might have seemed all continental

charm and effortless good looks to you, but it was just a shell. A sham. He was an animal. A beast.

"I blame Rita Marley."

"You keep saying that. What on earth do you mean, Tante?" Finally, she had my full attention. I put the sheets down and looked her in the face.

"Rita Marley. She let Bob do whatever the hell he wanted. She even sang backup on 'Stir It Up', for God's sake. What more humiliation could there be than for a man's wife to sing on the song he wrote for his outside woman? And yet, there she was, oohing and ahhing as that bastard sang a love song for another woman."

The glass in Tante's hand was shaking now.

"And when you confront them about their stinking whores, they beat you on top of it . . . No woman no cry, my ass."

She let go of the glass. It shattered, bathing my feet in splinters and gin.

"Tante?" I knocked on her bathroom door. She'd locked herself in. I could hear her bawling through the thin plywood layers.

"Just go away, darling. I'll be all right," she said, in between howls.

I changed my clothes in the laundry room, having swept away the shards of crystal and wiped up the spilled liquor.

On my way out, I stopped to glance in on Uncle Peter. Again, he gripped my hand. "Abby."

I shook my head gently; again, prised his hand off mine.

I let myself out.

Just as I climbed into my car, I heard music turned up loud. It was Bob Marley singing "Stir It Up".

ON THE EDGES OF HISTORY

Judy Raymond

"My life is a daily manifestation of miracles," said Arthur Raymond, walking through his family's house on Borde Street, then a middle-class area on the outskirts of Port of Spain, a lively, ramshackle city where neat homes and cocoa-planters' grander houses rubbed shoulders with barrack-yards or stood within sight of appalling slums.

He was a devout Catholic, but that was still a surprising thing for him to say. Because sometimes there were what seemed like miracles; but there was also terrible sadness, and sometimes the two mingled in a way you wouldn't believe possible. Given his early years, too, it was unexpected that he would view his life as miraculous.

Still, it seemed natural that this story about Arthur Raymond, my grandfather, should begin and end with his faith, because it seemed to have sustained him through desolate times; and because one of his daughters stressed how devout he was; and because those of his children who talked to me when I asked about him were so reverential, as though he were a saint

The miraculous was combined with the unbearable in 1936,

blighted because it was the year Myra — his fourth daughter and seventh child — died, aged ten, of rheumatic fever.

But just after her death, Arthur won the sweepstake with a ticket whose numbers Myra had chosen. This $66,000 windfall saved him from financial ruin, and even allowed him, then in his forties, to buy the house on Borde Street, rather than continuing to rent.

That was also the year when the Privy Council in London, the highest court of the colony of Trinidad and Tobago, ruled on an appeal by Raymond's employer and editor, A.P.T. Ambard of the *Port of Spain Gazette*. The Privy Council found Ambard not guilty of contempt of court on account of an editorial in the paper, in a judgment that has been used to defend the freedom of the press around the Commonwealth ever since. According to family history and popular belief, Arthur Raymond wrote the editorial. But he didn't, as his own notes told me.

As for his devotion to his Catholic faith, well, we're all sinners, and some of his descendants don't share his beliefs; but his immaculate image as a pious family man has also been brought into question by the reminiscences of one of the few people still alive who knew him.

It would never have occurred to Arthur Raymond to produce any kind of autobiography; he was a self-effacing man, as you can tell from the surviving copies of a very few of his letters, typewritten — without errors — on onion-skin paper. He considered himself unremarkable. In fact, he often felt himself a failure; and his accomplishments and good qualities weren't perhaps as extensive as his children wanted to believe. But his story sheds light on the lives of many black people of the early twentieth century who worked their way up despite huge obstacles. It's his ordinariness, and what he achieved nevertheless, that make my grandfather's story an illuminating one.

II

It begins with Arthur because he is the first Raymond of whom anyone has memories.

By the time he was six, in 1898, his father was dead, at thirty-one. His mother, Cecilia Emelie de Gannes Raymond, was left pregnant, aged thirty, to raise their children alone. The sixth, Augustus, was named after the father who died before he was born. So Arthur's daughter Ursula, when I talked to her about him many years ago, said Augustus Junior, known in those days of patois as Ogiste, was "both Daddy's brother and his son": that is, Arthur had to help bring up his baby brother.

Arthur was the third child, but by the age of twenty he had lost his father, his eldest brother, and both his sisters. He was tall, dark, thin, and everyone who talked to me about him described him as "serious." His remaining older brother, Andrew, might have been expected to step into their father's shoes, but may have been mentally fragile: he was dead at thirty-six in 1927. Andrew was said to have taken his own life, swept away by the currents of depression and anxiety that pulled at the family and sometimes dragged them under.

The Raymonds had come to town from Cedros, where Augustus Papillon Raymond owned an estate. He was a cocoa merchant, and no doubt the family home at 66 East Dry River was in a respectable area, even though it was behind the bridge. East Port of Spain became known for its slums and crowded barrack yards, but it had also housed communities of free Africans during the nineteenth century; and in the early part of the twentieth, its foothills sheltered genteel but impoverished black and coloured people like Haynes, the protagonist of C.L.R. James's novel *Minty Alley* — and my great-grandmother.

Cecilia de Gannes Raymond may have been from south Trinidad

too: there is a De Gannes Village in southwest Trinidad, and a branch of the French Creole de Gannes family owned the Columbia Estate in Cedros. Not that Cecilia had any claim to it. She and the other black de Gannes may have got their name through descent from an illegitimate member of the family, though there was no sign in Cecilia's dark complexion that she was of mixed race. It's also possible that her ancestors and Augustus's — they were not many generations removed from slavery — may have been of pure African heritage and were simply given the names of the white families on whose estates they laboured.

There's one photograph of Cecilia, a stately, sturdy-looking young black woman. It's a studio portrait, and she is seated in an ornately carved chair against a faded backcloth, flanked by two of her children. She is wearing a dark, elaborate high-necked dress with mutton-chop sleeves, and a complicated hat with a tall, stiff bow. One hand holds her gloves in her lap; the other rests on the arm of her chair, showing the long fingers she passed down to so many of her descendants, along with her slenderness and height. She looks resolutely into the camera with big, clear eyes under a smooth brow; not quite smiling, but with more confidence and serenity than her children. The nervy, anxious Raymond temperament may have come from her husband's family, or may have been triggered by the trauma of the early deaths and the hardship that affected at least two generations. But perhaps by now Cecilia herself has weathered her husband's horribly early death, and feels she can raise their children decently; she can afford to dress them and herself with some style, if only for this formal portrait.

Cecilia had a sister, tall and thin like her, who also lived in Port of Spain: Lucina Pollard, "Tanty Na" to her nephews and nieces. She was a childless widow, and perhaps she helped Cecilia deal with her family, practically and financially.

Much of the sparse reliable information that can be gleaned

about the family from this period comes from surprisingly large bundles of paperwork dealing with their grave plots in Lapeyrouse Cemetery. This was the sole real property Cecilia left — worth $120 — when she died at fifty-four. Her husband and the three children who died before her were all buried there. On Cecilia's death, in 1922, the grave sites passed to Augustus, even though he was her youngest child. For Augustus Senior and Cecilia had been married only in 1896, at the Roman Catholic Cathedral of the Immaculate Conception. They already had three children, but under the law in those days, children were only legitimate if at the time of their birth their parents were legally married. Hence when Cecilia died, the grave plots went to Augustus, her only surviving legitimate heir.

Augustus had no children, and gave the plots informally to Arthur. That wasn't good enough: affidavits had to be sworn, letters of administration approved, the Port of Spain Corporation Ordinances adhered to, for the allotment to be officially transferred to Arthur's children. Thus all the forms and certificates and explanations staking their claim to a few square feet of earth.

The cemetery plots had an added importance because for more than a decade they were the only real estate Arthur owned. Until Myra helped him win the sweepstake, he and his wife and their ever-growing family were crammed into a series of rented houses around the city.

C.L.R. James, eight years younger, recorded in *Beyond a Boundary* what those times were like for lower-middle-class black boys. James was lucky. His grandfather had been a pan-boiler on a sugar estate, a skilled job and one by then usually held by white men. So he had "raised himself above the mass of poverty, dirt, ignorance, and vice which in those far-off days surrounded the islands of black lower-middle-class respectability like a sea ever threatening to engulf them." James's family owned their house and even had tenants.

In those days, the government offered free "exhibitions" from elementary schools to the two secondary schools, the state-owned Queen's Royal College and the Roman Catholic's St Mary's. There were only four exhibitions a year for boys who couldn't afford the fees. "Through this narrow gate boys, poor but bright, could get a secondary education and in the end a Cambridge Senior Certificate, a useful passport to a good job," writes James. The luckiest and the cleverest could then compete for three annual island scholarships to university in Britain, and study law or medicine. But as the journalist George John later put it, more bluntly, for young black men of that generation, unless you won a scholarship, "You were dead."

James explains, "The higher posts in the Government, in engineering and other scientific professions, were monopolised by white people, and, as practically all big business was in their hands, the coloured people were, as a rule, limited to the lower posts."

Eric Williams, born in 1911, wrote in his autobiography, *Inward Hunger,* that to get ahead, "The necessary social qualifications were colour, money, and education." His account of his family's lack of all three has an understandably bitter tone. His father was in a similar position to Arthur Raymond: dark in complexion, he had only a primary-school education, no money, and had to haul himself up by his bootstraps. Having a large family didn't help. The Williamses had the same number of children as my grandparents — twelve — though two of the Raymonds' children died young and they had a stillborn daughter. Williams's father, George, did not rise as high as Arthur Raymond; he worked for the post office from seventeen until he retired in 1935. The Raymonds, whichever of them had managed to acquire their cocoa estate, had done as well as James's family, until Augustus died.

Arthur Raymond went to Nelson Street Boys' School, but had no chance of a secondary education, though his father had a relative — a brother? — who was a teacher, Arthur Napoleon Raymond. Somehow, a way was found for Arthur's younger brother Augustus to become a book-keeper or accountant. But Arthur's own formal schooling ended when he passed his fourth-year examination, though he stayed on afterwards as a pupil-teacher. According to a job application he wrote many years later, he was a student telegraph operator for the Railway Department for a while; and he spent a year as a correspondence clerk with a leading firm of lawyers, J.D. Sellier & Co.

III

Arthur may have left J.D. Sellier to follow his heart. He became a journalist, working first for the *Argos*. Aldric Lee Lum had founded the paper in 1911, upsetting some members of his family, the Chinese community, and other conservative sectors of society, because his progressive newspaper was held to have positively socialist leanings. Writing about the Chinese in Trinidad, Walton Look Lai says the *Argos* played a key role in the early post-1918 labour movement; Bridget Brereton writes that, like Marcus Garvey's *Negro World*, it advocated "race pride," and local whites considered it seditious and wanted it suppressed.

While at the *Argos*, Arthur Raymond personally came to official notice, in his mid-twenties. Governor Sir John Chancellor had banned the use of masks for Carnival during World War I. The *Port of Spain Gazette* at this period frowned severely on Carnival, regarding it as an excuse for the rowdy lower classes — and disguised, depraved members of the upper ones — to get on immorally, their identities safely hidden. So the *Gazette* argued that the ban on masks should be made permanent. The *Argos*, "the people's paper," responded by lampooning the *Gazette*, "that tottering and imbecile old lady of St Vincent Street."

The *Gazette* went further, campaigning for not only masks but

Carnival itself to be banned. But the *Argos* had argued for years that the festival should simply be reorganised and higher standards of costume and behaviour encouraged, and continued to deride the *Gazette* as the "mouthpiece of the rump of the old proprietor class." By now the *Argos*, by contrast, had come to be identified with Captain Cipriani's Trinidad Workingmen's Association.

The issue came to a head after the war ended in 1918. The *Guardian* (which had begun publication in 1917) sided with the *Gazette*. The *Argos*, however, called for a week of "victory Carnival" celebrations, as a reward for the returning troops, and because there had been no proper festivities during the war. Then a fundamentalist Christian group sent a petition against Carnival to Governor Chancellor. So the *Argos* organised its own petition, to be presented to the Governor by a deputation including several prominent black citizens — city councillor Dr A.C. McShine; the radical lawyer Emmanuel Mzumbo Lazare (once a leader of the Ratepayer's Association, which led the Water Riots of 1903, when the Red House was set on fire); and the Frederick Street merchant Aldwin Maillard. Arthur F. Raymond was secretary to the deputation (and by now editor of the *Argos*; despite his lack of schooling, he was a bright young man and an autodidact).

On the appointed date, some members were suddenly unable to attend. Or, as Arthur put it in a magazine article forty years later, "Several members . . . proved less eager to confront the formidable and domineering Chancellor than they had been to join the deputation. Some were absent on the morning . . . group pressure had to be brought to bear on others." (Lazare was missing, and defected to the *Guardian's* side when it called for an uptown Carnival in the Savannah, rather than the downtown festival the *Argos* supported.)

Worse, the Governor decided the unfortunate young Raymond — the most junior group member and hence possibly the easiest to intimidate — and the broker J.M. Wharton were "the two agitators." He also warned that he would hold the delegation's members personally responsible if there were any disorder during Carnival. Raymond was actively threatened: Chancellor "emphasised [this]," wrote my grandfather, "by shaking his finger into the faces of some of the delegates, including the poor Secretary upon whom he further impressed his personal responsibility."

Arthur survived this alarming literal encounter with the long arm of the colonial authorities. Carnival proceeded as the delegation had asked, after the members went about lecturing the populace about being on their best behaviour.

But the days of the *Argos* were numbered. After the paper closed in 1919 or 1920, Arthur found himself, ironically, knocking on the door of the same *Port of Spain Gazette* that his previous paper had labelled a "tottering and imbecile old lady."

Actually, though the *Gazette* is now generally considered to have functioned as the conservative mouthpiece of the ruling classes, it wasn't always that simple. In Arthur Raymond's time, it was edited and part-owned by Andre Paul Terence Ambard, who, though he had an impeccably French Creole name, came from a coloured branch of the family, and whose mansion on Queen's Park West had been repossessed in 1919. The left-wing British writer Arthur Calder-Marshall found that "The Labour movement has a greater belief in the *Port of Spain Gazette* than in its rival, because Mr Ambard has shown willingness to give Labour a hearing in his paper."

As a newspaperman, Ambard was admirably independent. George John recalled, for instance, that if an advertiser complained about the newspaper's stance on an issue, Ambard would hand back his advertisement and tell the disgruntled client he was free to take his custom elsewhere.

In 1932, there was a dispute between the *Gazette* and Colonial Secretary Howard Nankivell, because it published information from official documents without asking permission. Nankivell told the *Gazette* that until it promised to stop, "all facilities heretofore granted to representatives from your paper of visiting Government offices and interviewing Government officers have been withdrawn."

Ambard replied that if the other two dailies had already given such assurances, that was "a matter of supreme indifference to me. They are free to conduct their papers in any manner they wish." But such action against a single paper would not be allowed to rest quietly, he said. The matter was eventually settled — but only after the *Gazette* published all eight letters between Ambard and Nankivell, and Arthur Raymond wrote two editorials, published on 23 and 30 October respectively, on "The Liberty of the Press" and "The Liberty to Publish."

The diplomat J. O'Neil Lewis was once a reporter at the *Gazette*, and sixty years later, in a letter to the editor of another paper, he praised the "fearless and indomitable" A.P.T. Ambard and "his chief leader-writer, the renowned Arthur Raymond." They were, he wrote, "ever on the alert to repel any attempt at interference with their collection and publication of, and forthright comment upon, the news occurring daily."

He referred specifically to the editorial the *Gazette* was bold enough to publish on 29 June, 1934: "The Human Element," comparing the sentences imposed in two court cases apparently involving attempted murder (the *Gazette* reported extensively on both, but was vague about the actual charges). In one, a police bandsman was accused of shooting at the bandmaster. He admitted to being surprised that the bullet passed harmlessly through his victim's shirt.

In the other, a boat captain, John Sheriff, meant to kill the woman he lived with, whom he suspected of being unfaithful. Instead he mistakenly slashed a complete stranger, a Mrs Pearl Busby, with a razor. She was horribly mutilated and lost the baby she was carrying.

The court sentenced bandsman Joseph St Clair to eight years' imprisonment; Sheriff got seven years. The *Gazette* commented on "how greatly the personal or human element seems to come into play," citing public opinion that the former sentence was "as unduly severe as the other was lenient." It hastened to add that the decisions were at the judges' discretion, and it was certainly not suggesting that one was habitually more lenient than the other.

But the courts took a dim view of the paper's expressing any opinion on the issue, and Ambard — who may have written the editorial, and was in any case held responsible for it as the paper's publisher — was found in contempt and ordered to pay a fine of £25 or serve a month's imprisonment. He appealed — and in 1936 the Law Lords overturned the decision. Not only that, Lord Atkin handed down a ruling which was widely reported around the Empire, and has been used by the media ever since in defence of press freedom. "The path of criticism is a public way," Atkin decreed. "The wrong headed are permitted to err therein . . . Justice is not a cloistered virtue. She must be allowed to suffer the scrutiny and respectful even though outspoken comments of ordinary men."

Decades later, J. O'Neil Lewis wrote that the editorial in question was "confidently believed to have been written by Raymond." But Arthur Raymond kept a notebook, which I still have, that lists every one of the 1,722 editorials he wrote for the *Gazette* between 1931 and 1940. "The Human Element" isn't in it. So there went his place in history. (He had, however, written an 11 June editorial on the bandmaster case, which perhaps partly inspired the later one. It commented on the "unusual number of interventions from the Bench," and noted that the accused suffered racial taunts from the bandmaster (both were black); but then — in contrast to Raymond's usual elegance and directness — it strayed into arguments about the accused man's syphilis, and whether it had been properly treated. "It is unthinkable," the paper fumed in a rather alarmist manner, "that a man known to have a contagious disease . . . should be allowed to roam at large.")

Editorials in those days could be as long as 1,200 words, and my grandfather took their writing very seriously. Many of his papers, now held at the University of the West Indies, St Augustine, must have been background information for them: official reports on aspects of life in the colony, such as the water situation, or public health, or statistical digests. In 1939 he asked Ambard if he could write no more than three editorials a week: until then he had to research and write them at home almost every night, because his office duties as deputy editor did not allow time to write them there. He acknowledged that this would affect his income, but also said the state of his health required him to cut back on his working hours.

He also wrote at least some of the *Gazette's* (unsigned) reports on the June–July 1937 strikes, which started in the southern oilfields and spread as far as Tobago estates. Much of the information came from official sources, as telephone communications were cut, and the government imposed censorship on news from the oil belt. Even a report on the Legislative Council's debate on a proposed pay rise for government workers had to be taken from an official transcript. But Raymond was praised for his coverage by the Governor, Sir Murchison Fletcher, who professed sympathy for the workers, oversaw negotiations with employers, pushed for an inquiry into working conditions, and whom the *Gazette* commended for his "untiring" mediation efforts. (Fletcher and his Colonial Secretary, Nankivell, also highly regarded by the working classes, were resented by the elites, and, shortly after, were abruptly forced out of office. Nankivell may even have been driven to suicide; he fell — or threw himself — from a train in Europe in 1938.)

Later, Raymond was involved with the *Clarion*, a weekly working-class paper that appeared for several years after World War II, and to which the Trinidad-born pan-Africanist George Padmore was a regular contributor.

IV

But Arthur didn't stay in journalism for the rest of his career. In 1940 he sent a brief but successful application to the Colonial Secretary, John Huggins, saying he had heard the Government needed assistance in the Information Officer's Department. He went on to become Information Officer, and may have been the first local to hold the post, which no doubt paid better than journalism. As a black man, he would not have been made editor of the *Port of Spain Gazette*.

By now he was in his late forties, well respected and influential; my aunt Ursula later described him as "the first local consultant," because so many people came to him for advice. Albert Gomes, writer, politician, and trade unionist, was one of them. He campaigned against the censorship of calypso and the ban on Shouter Baptists, and supported steelpan and the Little Carib Theatre. His friends included C.L.R. James and the writers Alfred Mendes and Ralph de Boissière.

Raymond was on friendly terms with C.L.R. James. Lennox Pierre, lawyer, trade unionist, and political activist, was his godson. Seepersad Naipaul, a fellow journalist who worked across the street from the Gazette at the *Guardian,* presented "Mr A.F. Raymond" with an inscribed copy of his self-published 1943 book *Gurudeva and Other Indian Tales.* Raymond knew George John, the West Indies fast bowler, and hence George Junior, another *Guardian* reporter. He took an interest in young George's career, and would talk to him about their profession. George's father took him to visit Raymond occasionally, at his home, and later at the Information Office, a wooden building on the grounds of the Red House, where the eternal flame is now.

It was said in the family that when Eric Williams set out on the journey that took him to Oxford and eventually to Whitehall, the send-off for him was held at my grandparents' house. They were friendly with Williams's parents, who lived nearby; the two couples had much in common.

By now some of Arthur's own children had civil service jobs; several later went away on government scholarships. He had been married since 1918 or 1919, to Eulalie Feon (or Fionne) McGrath, and their twelve children were born between then and 1937. Sonny (FitzAlbert) was the first, in June 1919; the last living child was Felix, born in 1932.

My grandmother was slender and beautiful. She was fair-skinned — coloured, as they said then: she had French and Irish blood, and her father Emile McGrath had come from St Martin, her mother, Mary Chabrol, from Guadeloupe. In the few photos of her, she is big-eyed and solemn, perhaps even sad, giving little away. She was diabetic, and as with Eric Williams's mother Eliza, bearing all those children — and running a huge household, even with some hired help — must also have taken a toll on her. She died at sixty-five; her gravestone records her as a "self-sacrificing mother, a dutiful wife . . . called to her eternal rest" in 1957. Those were, I suppose, the things one said in those days about wives and mothers, but looking back now, they seem formulaic, almost grudging. My aunts and uncles didn't talk much about her, whereas they worshipped their father. I can't help thinking, "But what about her? Was she happy? Did she get what she wanted? What was she like? Am I imagining the sadness in her face?" I wonder how much of her husband's emotions she had to cushion and carry, and whether she shared his deep religious faith. Three of her children died young. Her daughters all worked, even though all but one had children. Her own children never mentioned her working even at home to help support the family; perhaps she filled her time by mending and letting out clothes for them, or worrying about stretching the housekeeping money to feed four sons and five daughters, plus her husband's fatherless niece Evelyn, whom they had taken in. For all the esteem in which my grandfather was held, only for a few years at the end of his career could he have come close to being well paid. And there may have been another reason for her apparent sadness.

V

Ferdie Ferreira is a raconteur, man about town, longtime PNM insider, and a former dock worker who became acting general manager of the port. Born in 1932, he's also a man who knew everyone and has a brilliant memory. He knew the man he refers to as "Arthur Faustin Raymond," and describes him as one of the more respected black members of the community, even calling him "upper-class."

By contrast, Ursula described her father as having "a string band of children, with not a cent to his name." Sometimes he feared he would be "engulfed" by that "mass of poverty, dirt, ignorance, and vice" he saw around him in the city's slums and barrack yards.

But, although he has an exaggerated view of Arthur Raymond's social status, financial situation, and academic qualifications, Ferdie Ferreira also knows something about my grandfather that casts him in another, very different light.

Ferreira knew the Raymonds from when he was about ten, when they lived at 15 Borde Street, the house bought with the miraculous sweepstake win. Captain Andrew Arthur Cipriani, trade unionist and politician, lived around the corner, on New Street; Arthur Raymond, says Ferreira, "would have known the gallant captain." The Ferreiras lived a block away on lower Dundonald Street, in a barrack yard, where whole families shared one room each, and a communal space for cooking and washing. These days Ferreira calls the area a ghetto.

Ferdie was a contemporary of the youngest Raymond, my late

uncle Felix. The middle-class boys were happy to escape the confines of middle-class life, and would sneak out to lime with the "ghetto boys" until they had to go home when darkness fell. They would suck mango together, and played cricket and football after school and at weekends — once their parents didn't find out. They didn't go to the same schools, but games in the Savannah were the great equaliser, says Ferreira. It was useful to know the better-off boys because they owned sports equipment. In return, the boys from the barrack yards would make out they were badjohns and offer protection in school "wars."

Arthur Raymond was always immaculate, with suit, hat, and umbrella, decent and polite. Ferreira didn't get to know him personally until about 1954, when he became a messenger boy for the POPPG — the Party of Political Progress Group, formed in 1947 and led by Raymond's acquaintance Albert Gomes. The larger-than-life Gomes came from Belmont, a lower-middle-class area, and was Portuguese; first brought to Trinidad as labourers, the Portuguese were not yet considered white.

When Ferreira came to work at the POPPG headquarters in the Gordon Grant building on Independence Square, my grandfather was the office manager. To Ferreira, the party was one of colonial capitalists; it was seen by then as representing the white business community — although Gomes was none of those things, and it also included black professionals. The messenger boy viewed Arthur Raymond in the same light as the party he worked for, though Raymond's journalistic career showed he wasn't as conservative as he seemed. But then, the young Ferreira was a Butlerite, and was falling under the spell of Eric Williams, whose People's National Movement wiped out the POPPG in its first election in 1956. (Gomes eventually joined the Democratic Labour Party, but then migrated; the POPPG is now almost completely forgotten.)

Ferdie Ferreira wasn't in the Raymonds' social class — he

would not have been welcome as a visitor in their home, he says without rancour — and Mr Raymond was his boss. But he ran errands for Arthur Raymond that told Ferdie something even Mr Raymond's family didn't know. Every now and again, Arthur would ask Ferreira, "very circumspect, 'Could you just drop this?'" — a small envelope that obviously contained money and was addressed to a lady on Pembroke Street, a Miss Harding. It didn't seem to be a family relationship, Ferreira says. He thinks Miss Harding may have been a nurse, and she lived with her sister and a niece or perhaps an adopted child, "not too far from the library, on the left-hand side, in some apartments there." She was decent and well spoken, advanced in age, not a young person, he recalls, a thick, dark woman. Young Ferdie didn't consider her attractive.

It's possible that my grandfather sent money for Miss Harding out of charity; perhaps she was a friend and the money was to help raise her niece. But in that case, one of Arthur's many children could have taken it for her. So Ferdie drew a different conclusion.

"The conduit for concubinage," he explains, "was the Friendly Societies." These were the forerunners of credit unions, whose main attraction was that for four cents a week or so, you could save towards a death benefit to cover the cost of a funeral; and you got a bonus at Christmas. After Friendly Society meetings, some gentlemen would go home with women who were not their wives; as Ferreira puts it, "They would do their damage in the night."

Among Arthur's personal papers — the typed-up prayers, the account book for 1946–47, the newspaper reports of the Ambard court victory, the lists of family births and deaths — is a certificate issued in 1953 by the Trinidad Verbena Friendly Society, listing Felix Raymond and Yvonne Wilson (the third Raymond daughter) as dependants of "Bro. Arthur F. Raymond." He may have belonged to other friendly societies as well; that was not uncommon. If Ferreira's assumptions are accurate, that might be where Arthur met Miss

Harding, and an alibi for further meetings. Ursula said her father would walk round the Savannah in the evenings before coming home with a pocket full of sweets or nuts. Perhaps he did, though that was a long detour from the *Gazette's* newsroom on St Vincent Street; it may also have been a way of accounting for some visits to his lady friend, if that was what she was.

VI

Arthur Raymond was a man of faith; he said his prayers in the gallery of the house every morning, and on the first Friday of each month he woke the whole family early for devotions to the Sacred Heart of Jesus. Every week he visited the family graves at Lapeyrouse to clean them and to pray for the souls of the departed.

His papers include a note recording that after her death, masses were said for his wife at Sacred Heart Church at 6.15 am on the second of every month throughout the year; and typed copies of a few prayers. One says in part: "Grant us . . . the courage to be true to our convictions . . . grant that our ambitions be modest . . . Grant us . . . the peace that dwells in a heart free of hate." Another begins: "Let me do my work each day, and if the darkened hours of despair overcome me, may I not forget the strength that comforted me in the desolation of other times . . . May I not forget that poverty and riches are of the spirit . . . And though age and infirmity overcome me and I come not within sight of the Castle of my dreams, teach me still to be thankful for life, and for time's golden memories that are good and sweet . . ."

These were prayers from the heart, but for long periods he felt they went unheard. Among Arthur's papers are letters that are startling in both their candour and their desperation.

In July 1958, he wrote to his former editor ("Dear Mr Ambard"), asking permission to publish selected editorials from the *Port of Spain Gazette,* and promising to visit to reminisce, "one of these dry afternoons when I happen to beat the wave of depression that has engulfed me recently . . ."

Eight years before, while he was still government information officer, he had written to a Mr Garner, a colleague who had called at his office that morning. The formality of his letters makes it hard to judge whether they were also friends. But this is the place in his surviving writings where you hear Arthur Raymond's voice most clearly. It begins like a business letter, then becomes a cry of pain.

"You little know," Arthur confessed, "how the words you uttered to me served as a stimulus in these my dark days of depression."

It is the mere truth to say that, measured in ordinary terms, in the sense of possession of this world's goods, my life has been an economic failure. In my 57th year, the outlook for me is bleak and dreary and therefore, not without mis-givings. It is therefore a measure of consolation to know that I happen, as you say, to enjoy the esteem of at least a few of my fellow-men who appear to appreciate the sacrifices and efforts I have made at trying to rear, to decent standards, a fairly large family.

. . . I have a great deal to be thankful for to Him above and to some of my friends who have never shut the door where my children are concerned. On the other hand, one's children are not investments, and it is neither right nor expedient to base one's economic future upon the possible future success of one's children . . .

It is in this setting that I say that life has no future for me; however, as I said above, the words which you uttered to me this morning have at least for the moment served to dispel the clouds of depression, and it is heartening to feel that one's life, judged even by the apparent success of one's children, has not been spent altogether in vain.

> Yours very sincerely,
> Arthur F. Raymond.

The letter is heartbreaking, however many times you read it. Arthur was not yet sixty; his wife was still alive; he owned a house; he had a respected and — in its field — reasonably well-paid job. And yet he battled for long years against near-overwhelming hopelessness: "life has no future for me." For him, despair would have been a sin against the Holy Ghost. Yet he may have been tempted to follow his brother Andrew's path; his faith may have held him back from stepping into the abyss, but he was drawn to its brink. He may have considered his terrible aloneness and emptiness a spiritual affliction; and in those days, even if he sought medical help for his depression, little or none would have been forthcoming.

Other than lack of financial success, and his early losses, what might have triggered it? Perhaps he wanted to be more politically active; but journalism and then a civil-service job wouldn't allow that. He may have had ambitions to be a writer, like his near-contemporaries Mendes and James. Among his papers is the draft of a radio talk on his impressions of London. He had gone there in the late 1940s, for four months, while he was information officer, spending some time at the Colonial Office — and twenty-nine days in St Mark's, a cancer hospital in Harrow. The radio piece is unremarkable except for the depth of his gratitude for the kindness he received from English people; perhaps he had spent so many years as a journalist, trying to record the facts dispassionately, that he couldn't access the emotion and the imagination needed to bring his writing to life. And journalism — the time it demands, the endless bad news, the persnickety corrections and fact-checking — can be soul-destroying. At any rate, the contrast between his measured public writings and the raw misery of his outpouring to "Mr Garner" couldn't be greater.

When Arthur retired in 1952, a former Governor, Sir John Shaw, was among those who wrote to him, praising his sincerity, tact, and ability. Raymond also kept a letter from Mr Ferdinand, senior inspector of schools in Tobago, who imagined it must be "a source of great personal satisfaction to you to look back on your career dedicated to the service of your fellowmen, and marked with dignity and selfless-ness [sic] and calmness in the discharge of the onerous responsibility attaching thereto." They may have helped on his "dark days of depression."

My grandmother died in 1957, and some time later Arthur went to live with Ursula and her sons. Like some of my cousins, I have a dim memory of him: very tall, dark, and intimidating because he was so grave; even as a small child, like everyone who knew him, I recognised his underlying sadness. His children didn't refer to it, except obliquely: "Poor Daddy," said Ursula, giving me his account book: "He was always so careful."

Arthur wrote an account for the *Hummingbird* magazine in 1960 of the Carnival controversy of many years before. He wrote (unsigned) pieces for the *Radio Times* magazine until it ceased publication in 1964. He made some progress with his plan to publish collected editorials from the *Gazette*: the UWI collection includes what look like page proofs of many (not all written by him), including the triumphant "Fiat Justitia!" ("Let justice be done!") from after the 1936 Privy Council ruling.

One Saturday afternoon at the end of November 1965, while cleaning Ursula's car, Arthur was stung by a jack spaniard, and collapsed. He may have had a stroke, though his death certificate said it was colon cancer that killed him. He asked for a priest and his children. He died two days later at the Port of Spain General Hospital.

One friend wrote to my father that the country had lost one of its finest citizens, a patriot and a gentleman, a sterling character, a true Catholic and a model citizen. What more could one ask for?

Happiness, for one thing. My grandfather's story is sadder than I had thought, more complicated than the one I expected to tell, of a determined climb from difficult early circumstances to a position of respect, if not financial security. He never stopped worrying about money, nor believed he was successful, seeing himself with the warped, joy-sucking grey vision of those afflicted with depression. That susceptibility was the poisoned gift he couldn't help handing down, along with his height, the long fingers, his creativity, the high-strung temperament.

I visit my grandfather's grave occasionally. I don't pray, but I remember his prayer: ". . . if the darkened hours of despair overcome me, may I not forget the strength that comforted me in the desolation of other times . . ." and its wish to be able to find "time's golden memories . . . good and sweet."

I hope his prayer was granted and that he found peace.

TWO POEMS

Xavier Navarro Aquino

RETURNING FROM EXILE

Can be like suffocating in water. The soft popping
of the ears when the plane descends may soak the eyes
and the cold timbre tells us we should strap ourselves tighter
in order to ride down the final floors of troposphere, those last few
steps needed for landing. I pray: Safely, gently, and safely we go. As
    if singing
or humming might soon soothe you into death, if it happens. If I
    land, can I trace
the sides of my armrest just to feel anything? If I could pay a visit to
    the cemetery

and deliver those long overdue wreaths as if asking forgiveness for
    not calling

the night before you died. And when I do land and follow the tiles
    that work their way

past the rotating door out into the heat and air, I will look around
    me in that dark overpass,

the hot sun waiting at the margin, ready to argue with anyone who
    wants conversation,

the readiness of Spanish tongue twisting behind me, the light of
    the world never reaching

these shores, the island chorus blanketing the dry foothills near
    deserted beaches.

But there's nobody there to greet me. No kempt dresses
    meticulously steamed

in the morning, no joyful tears running down a face, staining a
    sky-blue guayabera

reminding me that it is still possible to weep and not be sad.

CONSTRUCTION OF STRUCTURE

It is an impossibility to want
but not need.
She sits on her round chair —
the librarian —
desk pampered with pamphlets and dusted books
marking binaries to catalogue experience, our own Berber woman
displaced in an artifice,
a room artificial and cold.

I wonder if I've seen enough strikes and poisoned books,
strikes that end with scattering bodies and the still frame,
composed letters and postcards singing the worn tooted horn,
books as insignia, proof that our story isn't told enough,
the stories told by my mother,
the green parrots singing by a city morgue
ruffling leaves
calling to each other
and how many women stay in silence
because they wish to not fight
the pigeons that fall dead
from inflated breasts,
the black boy no longer adorning breath.

The Julian calendar is still used,
buckled in the bar codes where steel currents are connected to
    humming robotics.
Eyes turned to scanners.
Mom says we are alight,
we are not animals,
we hide in the spines of dusted notes
written on the margins of opened pages
coded for Julian animals. Savaged by concrete wild.

Migration happens when we are abandoned.

I follow the Berber people to their stories,
crowns drawn on tamarind sands
woven frays and filament functioning as old marking.
Ask them about it and they will know
to follow the paths that trace ancestry through the Sahara.

Migrations happened, involuntarily.
Ask me about it

and I will tell.

THE ISLANDS OF MY LIFE

Diana McCaulay

Dreaming of islands — whether with joy or in fear, it doesn't matter — is dreaming of pulling away, of being already separate, far from any continent, of being lost and alone — or it is dreaming of starting from scratch, recreating, beginning anew.

— Gilles Deleuze, 1922

An island is not merely a geological feature. Islands have a mystique — they are symbols of separation, isolation, and adventure. An island is a place ripe for the conquering — literature is full of stories of the desert island, claimed and owned and ruled — its desertedness banished. Jamaica is not just an island — we are an archipelagic state, an island of islands. There are roughly sixty-five small islands and cays in our waters, islands writ small. A few are large enough for people to live on them, some no more than rocks or sandbanks in the sea. Some of our islands are ninety miles from the coast across treacherous seas; others are ten minutes from the mainland, easily accessible for a few hours at the beach.

These are the islands of my life.

There is a small nub of rock at the entrance to Blue Hole in Portland. You can paddle through the narrow space between it and the mainland, or you can go through the large entrance where the open sea flows into the lagoon. This rock may be too small to be dignified by the word "island," although it is surrounded by water, and it is not exactly a cay either, having no sandy beach. Yet it does have a crust of vegetation at the top, and birds and crabs do visit. My childhood friends, the San San boys, decided to capture it one day. No girls were allowed. They made a flag out of a mop stick and someone's old surfing long shorts — jammies, we used to call them — and they set off in one of the dinghies. I stood on the fishing beach and watched them laugh and skylark together. One of them stayed in the boat, hanging onto a convenient rock, and the others climbed to the top of the "island." I could see they were having difficulty planting the stick, but eventually they seemed to find a crevice and they anchored the flag, way past the vertical. It's not straight, I yelled at them from land. They gave no sign of hearing me.

I wanted to be part of the island-capturing expedition. Is it in our DNA, this wish to capture, to own an island surrounded by the sea, unoccupied by people except those chosen by us, a place we can be rulers? Rich people do it all the time — is there any greater sign of immense privilege than ownership of a private island? For myself, I was glad when the flag on the unnamed nub of rock at Blue Hole did not survive a single night — it remained uncaptured. Had I been the one to plant that flag, though, I suspect I would have been fine with my own claim.

Islands are ephemeral. Continental islands break off and drift away, oceanic islands rise from the depths, volcanoes start islands, hurricanes return them to sandbanks. There is a snapshot of another island on the bookshelf beside me — Tern Cay, or Needles Cay, as the fishermen called it. Tern Cay was off Needles Point — hence its nickname — near to Manatee Bay and Wreck Reef in what was to become the Portland Bight Protected Area. In the mid-1990s, before the protected area had been declared, I went with a new boyfriend, let's call him Joe, and a group of his huntin', fishin', and shootin' cronies to spend the weekend on nearby Pigeon Island.

We met at Morgan's Harbour, but the man who owned the boat was late. The men started drinking and night fell. I was the only woman present. Finally, the owner showed up and against the objections of the sober people — me and Joe — we cast off and headed for the Portland Bight cays. My father always told me — be careful who you go to sea with. As we left Morgan's Harbour, I knew I was taking a life-threatening risk.

The night was moonless, the sea was rough, and we were heading for Wreck Reef. There were two names that scared us as seagoing children — Farewell Buoy and Wreck Reef. The latter was a place where ships foundered on the sharpest of reefs. Until you got behind Wreck Reef, the waves were huge and the surge of the sea relentless. The green-blue glow of the boat's instruments illuminated the faces of the men who peered at them. At least they had stopped drinking. Surely, we would be okay, I told myself, this was a modern boat with a radio and a depth sounder and a many-horsepower engine. Perhaps it would be a long night, but we would be okay.

I watched the boat's wake and that was when I realised we would not be okay, because it was not streaming straight behind us. The foaming evidence of our path through the sea was a zig-zag and I knew then the captain had no idea where he was going. My father — keep a good lookout at sea, always. I went to the bow and held on tight as the boat rose and fell. Joe came with me, trying to persuade me to stay safe in the cabin.

I had not been there long when I saw the shine of breaking waves and a swirl of phosphorescence and I heard the crash of the waves on the reef. Wreck Reef, I bawled. Dead ahead! Come astern!

My words were whipped away by the wind and a wave took us closer. Joe ran for the bridge of the boat where the men were huddled; I heard his raised voice of warning and I held tight to the weather rail. The boat started to turn, the engines fighting the sea that heaved towards Wreck Reef. Too slow, I feared; too late.

We turned in time; the powerful boat engines did their job. I stayed on the bow and watched us leave Wreck Reef behind and eventually we were in its lee and the sea became much calmer. I was glad to have survived, and I was rigid with anger. The men were arguing. Take me to Old Harbour Bay, I shouted, to the captain and to Joe. I am not staying on this boat. You people are mad. The men tried to make light of what had happened but I could see they were shaken and now stone-cold sober.

We spent the night anchored in Old Harbour Bay, everyone sleeping where they could find a piece of deck. In the morning I said to Joe, I'm leaving.

I'm coming with you, he said. Don't go back to Kingston. Let's go to Little Pelican instead of Pigeon. We can spend the day and I'll get someone to come for us later.

How will we get to Pelican? I said.

I have a fishing canoe here, he said.

I told myself he was a good man to go to sea with.

We headed out with a tall, solid fisherman with a huge smile and a tendency to use Italian phrases because he had worked for some Italian contractors on the Old Harbour Bay power plant; we'll call him Carlton. It was early and the sea was calm. We hugged the coast past the two Goat Islands towards Needles Point, and then I saw a small sandy island with a single mangrove tree. What island is that? I asked.

Needles Cay, Carlton said.

Can we get there?

Not so easy to get through the reef, but sea is flat.

Joe was anxious to please. Let's go, he said.

And we went. Joe stood in the bow, gesturing as he saw the big coral heads, and Carlton slowly piloted the canoe through the encircling reef. We came into a sheltered area, calm, with a sand bottom, and the water that alluring turquoise that has brought generations of tourists to the Caribbean. I was enchanted, leaping out of the boat before we pulled it up on the beach, full of joy to leave the previous night's journey behind. The sand on the tiny island was white but coarse, which I would come to appreciate, because it did not blow around in high winds. The little mangrove tree gave shade. We spread our blanket on the sand, Carlton went to collect whelks for soup, and Joe and I lay together on Needles Cay.

For many years, we spent weekends on this small sandbank in the sea. Every time we went, we had to pick up garbage — plastic containers, juice boxes, glass bottles, old shoes, cigarette packs, fishing line — the modern-day flotsam of the sea. One Easter weekend, we built a shelter; or, more correctly, Carlton built a shelter while we gave design advice, using thatch palms from the mainland, me insisting that the thatch be cut from many palms, instead of a single one, so it would be a sustainable harvest, Carlton laughing at me and teasing me one day that rangers from NEPA, the environmental regulatory body, had accosted him. I was just beginning my environmental life then, just beginning to learn what the land could tolerate and what it could not. We roasted unscaled fish on a sheet of zinc, and made a sauce of seawater with scotch bonnet peppers, onions, limes, and pimento, and we ate with our fingers.

Needles Cay was always changing — its shape, its vegetation, the depth of the water. Seabirds I could not identify laid their eggs, and as the mangrove tree shed its leaves, a colony of soldier crabs began in the dry leaves and I could not imagine how the soldier crabs got there. The seabird eggs hatched and we watched the mother feed the fuzzy nestlings, screaming at us if we came too close. There were no mosquitoes or sandflies — the wind was too strong, the sand too coarse. We saw the island in all weathers. In a gale, when our boat broke anchor and left us huddling behind an inadequate tarpaulin, awaiting rescue. We saw it on calm days, when the sea slid over the sand like silk on skin, and we saw the changing canvas of the sky from watercolour dawns to oil-painted sunsets.

I saw how we changed things, no matter how careful we were. We poured our leftover drinking water on the mangrove tree and it grew healthier and stronger. The ants multiplied, gorging on the crumbs of our hard dough bread. We took friends there, my sister Suzie and her Italian boyfriend, Andrea, and we took my mother, who by then was not so agile and needed help getting in and out of the canoe, as I do now. Andrea shocked her the first time he saw Needles Cay by stripping naked and jumping into that clear water, just as I had done the first time I had seen it, although I had left my clothes on. The children of my family and friends called it Aunty D's island and they told me it spoiled them for other beaches.

We saw a single baby turtle hatchling fight its way to the sea late one afternoon. We saw night spear fishers come right up to the reef at night and during the years we went there, I saw the reef change. More algae, less live coral. Our shelter was used by others, probably fishermen, and we would see the remnants of cooking fires when we visited.

I have the photograph of Needles Cay on my shelf because it no longer exists. One weekend, we found the shelter burned to the ground and the mangrove tree scorched. No fence kept anyone out, the shelter was there for all to use, yet it angered someone enough to destroy it. Was it burned in a rage targeted at us — keep out, you uptown people — was it idle vandalism or simple carelessness? I wrote at the time that I feared the collective anger of our society, this lashing out, this undirected rage, this hatred of our land, this determination that someone or something should pay for our pain, even if that is a mangrove tree or a small coral cay. I wove my time on Needles Cay into my third novel, as a tribute and a record.

After the shelter was burned down, Joe and I did not go back to Needles Cay, because it did not seem safe anymore, and later our relationship ended. In 2004, Hurricane Ivan took Needles Cay and now it is a submerged sandbank, still surrounded by reef, more degraded than ever, I imagined, until recently when I saw a hopeful report about the state of the coral reefs around Tern Cay, with higher coral cover than the regional standard. It seemed faint praise. I stare at my photograph of Needles Cay when I want to remind myself of the fragility and impermanence of islands.

Islands can be places of revelry; places of forgetting. Every year there is a party on Maiden Cay, one of the Port Royal cays, off the Palisadoes, on the doorstep of the city of Kingston. Maiden Cay was my favourite of this set of small islands when I was a child, as although it was a sandbank without shade, the reef around it shimmered and the water shaded from navy blue to aqua in a thousand hues. When I learned to scuba dive, I dived on the spooky nearby shipwreck, called the *Cayman Trader*. Maiden Cay is now a party venue, and photographs of the biggest parties are posted on Facebook. There are so many people and boats that the island itself is hidden. There are jokes about not letting the International Monetary Fund see the pictures, because then they will know for sure Jamaica is not a poor country, given the enormous size of the boats broadcasting the wealth of their owners. In the photographs, the party people hold drinks in paper cups and many of those cups end up in the sea. Baby turtles have hatched during the parties.

Maiden Cay, Lime Cay, Rackham Cay, Gun Cay, Drunkenman's Cay, Southeast Cay — all are now part of the Palisadoes/Port Royal Protected Area, which, as environmental management has unfolded in Jamaica, is a term without meaning. "Protected Area" is just something to put on a sign and have a workshop about. I'm fond of telling my audiences that we'd put a nuclear plant in a protected area.

We build microcosms of our societies on islands. Robinson Crusoe constructed his world from his foundered ship, and gave orders to his slave, Man Friday. Of the novel, still assigned reading for students today, Gilles Deleuze wrote: God knows his people, the hardworking honest type, by their beautiful properties, and the evil doers by their poorly maintained shabby property. Robinson's companion is not Eve, but Friday, docile towards work, happy to be a slave, and too easily disgusted by cannibalism. Any healthy reader would dream of seeing him eat Robinson.

In 2007, my friend Esther Figueroa began documenting work by The Nature Conservancy's Jamaica Programme on the Pedro Bank and Cays. Pedro, as it is known, is a large submarine bank about ninety miles southwest of Jamaica, which breaks the surface in five places, two small rocks and three cays — Top Cay, Middle Cay, and Bird Cay are the common names of the cays. Jamaicans live on Top Cay and Middle Cay, and it is the existence of these permanent residents that allows Jamaica to claim archipelagic status and a much larger Exclusive Economic Zone than would otherwise be the case. Esther was filming the establishment of a new fish sanctuary at Pedro. Every few months or so, she went with a team to Middle Cay on a Jamaica Defense Force (JDF) Coast Guard boat, and she came back full of stories. She'd say, come and look at my footage, and I would visit her to look at the Dante-esque images of the living conditions on the Pedro Cays. What she told me: D, we have replicated our society out there. There is downtown, near to a burning garbage dump, there is mid-town, with better quality dwellings and shops, and there is uptown, with the concrete buildings of The Nature Conservancy and the JDF Coast Guard, set somewhat apart, even with a bit of greenery and a straggly coconut tree.

It was Esther's footage of booby birds holding their ground near the burning trash fires that galvanised me. I organised a media trip to the Pedro Cays on a JDF helicopter. We got there on a clear morning, a forty-five-minute trip, and I loved being on the helicopter, loved the moment when it floated free of the earth, it reminded me of swinging my leg over my horse or bicycle and becoming instantly a creature of movement.

The islands of the Pedro Bank rose from the sea, and the helo took us around once before we landed. The wind kicked up by the helo blades sent plastic bags flying and I knew they would end up in the sea. The helo settled to earth and I saw the booby birds, with their strange goat eyes and Zorro mask, on the ground so close to where we landed. They did not fly away. Those are tough birds, I said. The media folks had not noticed them.

Middle Cay was above all things an island, and I smelled the sea breeze and heard the waves and saw the encircling sea and my spirits lifted, despite everything else that populated that island — the mean dwellings, the wrecked toilets at one end of the cay, the place on the beach where the hundreds of people who lived on Middle Cay used as a latrine, the single standing toilet, painted pink, with a lock on the door. There was a murky pond near to where we stood. Garbage floated in it, and I later learned that it had been the excavation for the removal of guano, some short-lived economic opportunity, perhaps riches for someone. And there was the garbage dump, much bigger than I had imagined, testimony to the real essence of human beings, the evidence of our willingness to foul even the places where we live and say we love.

I walked around with the media teams. They spoke to people, they filmed the birds, the burning garbage, the brightly coloured fishing canoes, the waves coming in and out. The people talked of huge rats and lack of water and decades of government promises. A woman threw fish guts onto the beach and shrieking seabirds descended and the camera people aimed their cameras. The dwellings were haphazardly built, creating a series of convoluted lanes, and it was easy to feel lost, except that I knew a few steps in any direction would bring me to a view of the sea.

I talked with one fisher in a hammock, not a young man, well-fed, wearing only shorts. The hammock was strung in a shed, with a dark room behind it. The room's plywood wall had a square hole cut into it, a window of sorts, and I thought about our wish to confine and constrain the vistas our eyes can see, to put ourselves behind a wall of some kind, however flimsy, and gaze out through a window, preferably one that can be closed against the acts and sights of nature. The man swung gently in the breeze and he smoked a cigarette, there in the shade he had built. The journalists asked him about life on the Pedro Cays and he said he preferred it to the mainland, and for that moment, I could see why.

A few nights later, I was a guest on a TV programme with the Minister of Agriculture and Fisheries and the Acting Chief Executive Officer of the Fisheries Division. Cliff Hughes, the host and one of Jamaica's senior journalists, showed the damning images and the government officials made their excuses and promises. At the end of the programme, I was asked to give the last word and I looked at the camera and said that I wanted to speak directly to the people on the Pedro Cays. I knew they would be watching some small TV in a bar with power provided by a noisy, smelly generator. I said to them, the situation on the Pedro Cays cannot continue, and afterwards

I laughed at myself, because I knew the people of the Pedro Cays would themselves have been amused at this uptowner who visited them one day on a helo, for an hour or so, and told them what could or could not continue.

Of course, the situation on the Pedro Cays could and did continue. The media coverage was all I could have wished for, three weeks of stories and pictures and radio interviews, and there were high-level meetings and many promises made. A cleanup was done, funds were promised for regular cleanups, but no one thought it necessary to consider rules about how garbage would be handled on the Pedro Cays, so the cleanups were always poorly done and became less and less regular. The people on the Cays spoke of corruption and stopped helping. A handful of fishers were removed for not having the correct licenses and a few unoccupied shelters were demolished. A carrying capacity study was commissioned and done by the University of the West Indies, and I went to the stakeholder workshop that delivered the findings. As is nearly always the case with such studies and workshops, the PowerPoint presentations told us little we did not already know.

Now, the numbers of people living permanently on the Cays are high once more, the garbage collection has ceased, and the trash is being burned again. The booby birds still fight for space to lay their eggs and rear their young amid the fires. The Jamaica Environment Trust (JET), the small non-profit agency I founded, had a patrol boat out there for a year to make sure the fish sanctuary around Bird Cay (where I have never been) is monitored. Every now and then, fishers are arrested for fishing in the sanctuary, and they always say they did not know where they were, these men who can find a dot of an island in the middle of the Caribbean Sea at night. Mostly, the legal cases are thrown out; sometimes, a judge applies a miniscule fine. The Bird Cay fish sanctuary is less than 0.2 percent of the Pedro Bank — but not even a space so insignificant in area can be truly protected.

•

Islands arouse our impulses to journey afar, to conquer and to take. When Joe and I left Old Harbour Bay for Needles Cay, we would motor past the two Goat Islands. Great Goat Island was so large it looked like part of the mainland unless you were close to it. When the weather was bad, we would go between the two Goat Islands and the coast because it was sheltered there. I only remember going onto the Goat Islands once — when my Canadian nephews got sunburned while on Needles Cay. Carlton took us to Great Goat Island because there was sinkle bible — aloe vera — there, and he pulled up the canoe to a rocky bare place on the shore, and he disappeared into the thickest bush. I tried to follow him but it was too hard. We waited in the canoe, our heads bowed in the sun, and Carlton came back with thick stems of aloe which he squeezed onto the arms and necks of the sunburned white children. Then, I did not recognise high-quality forest or healthy mangroves or the productive shallow inshore waters because I knew little about them and was not yet fully aware how much at risk they were.

So I cannot declare time spent on the Goat Islands — they were just there, part of a coastline that had not yet been developed for hotels or roads or airports, a feature that we went past to get to another, less inhospitable island.

Sometime in April 2013, I was at a party and, as had become the norm for my that-environmental-woman persona, I was approached by an acquaintance wanting to give me information. He said that "Chinese people" were crawling all over the Goat Islands. By then, China was our official development partner and had done much road-building and road-fixing and the seawalls of the Palisadoes and various bridges and a stadium (now rotting in the sun) and many blue and white signs (now rusting) proclaiming their contribution to Jamaica's national development. Over the next few months, I heard rumours of various developments planned for the Goat Islands, but none of my painstakingly constructed government sources knew anything. There was nothing to do but wait.

The Goat Islands are — were — featured in Jamaica's National Biodiversity Strategy and Action Plan — they were to be declared a sanctuary for our critically endangered iguana. Iguanas used to be on the Goat Islands — the last one was seen on Great Goat in the 1940s. Little Goat had been cleared for a US seaplane base in World War II and someone decided that islands named for goats should have goats on them, so goats were introduced. End of iguanas.

Apart from the scientists who studied them and the international groups that had poured money into the recovery of the Jamaican iguana (*Cyclura collei*), it seemed to me that only one person cared about the iguana — John Maxwell. John was a veteran journalist and he wrote often about the iguana story, how the Jamaican iguana was once widely distributed across the south coast, driven to presumed extinction by hunting, loss of habitat, and predation by the introduced mongoose and other predators, was rediscovered twice — once in 1970, by Dr Jeremy Woodley on an expedition to Hellshire, and then in 1990, by a feral pig hunter, Edwin Duffus, who rescued a mortally wounded iguana from his dogs. This 1990 rediscovery sparked new interest in searching for and protecting the Jamaican iguana. Dr Peter Vogel, a lecturer at the University of the West Indies, led the iguana recovery programme and John used to write about it, whenever the latest ill-conceived scheme to destroy the Hellshire forest became known. Jamaicans are seriously reptile-phobic and I used to wish John would focus on other environmental crimes, because I figured every time he defended a big ugly lizard, he lost support for the environment in a more general sense.

The essence of the iguana recovery programme was head-starting — taking hatchlings to the Hope Zoo and growing them to a size where they were less vulnerable to predation — and then releasing them back into the Hellshire forest. In addition, the team set traps to reduce the numbers of predators and the feral pigs that dug up nests and ate the eggs. Funding was provided by several zoos and international foundations, led by the Fort Worth and San Diego Zoos. Slowly, the numbers of releases increased and so did the number of breeding females and live hatchlings. The Jamaica iguana recovery programme was written up in the scientific literature and regarded by the international conservation community as a fantastic success; a model for programmes to reintroduce species into the wild.

Dr Vogel was murdered in 2007 at his home near the university campus. His helper and her common-law husband were convicted of the crime in June 2017. The crime was unconnected to his work with Jamaican iguana. The iguana recovery programme was taken over by an American, Dr (now Professor) Byron Wilson, who came to Jamaica in 1997 as Dr Vogel's post- doctoral fellow and settled here. By then, it was clear that the current programme would always be dependent on conservation funding. The removal of non-native species and predators on the two Goat Islands followed by the establishment of a sanctuary there for various endangered animals had been discussed in the 1960s, and then formalised by Dr Woodley in the early 1970s. The first meeting of the iguana recovery programme in 1993 settled on this as a primary objective. Having the Goat Islands as a sanctuary would mean much less money needed for predator control, and the islands could then themselves be the headstart facility, without the need for cages at the Hope Zoo in Kingston. All involved signed off on this objective and it became stated government policy in many documents, including the National Biodiversity Strategy and Action Plan. But the sanctuary was never declared by the Jamaican government.

Byron Wilson is a plain-speaking person, and he soon became frustrated with NEPA, which, as the Jamaican iguana was protected under the Wild Life Protection Act, had to approve the recovery programme, and even to be seen to be leading it. In 2012, Byron invited me to visit the iguana project, and although by then I had been diagnosed with having weak bones — from carrying the planet around, I told people, (it sounded more heroic than post-menopausal osteoporosis) — and warned not to fall down, I went. I convinced my husband, Fred, to come with me, in case I needed to be carried out. We went with the field team by boat from the Port Royal Marine Lab to Manatee Bay, retracing my childhood journeys to Wreck Reef and the cays of Portland Bight. Shuffle your feet, Byron told us as we prepared to disembark into the soft, murky sand of Manatee Bay. There are a lot of stingrays. I thought of my father then and his warnings about stingrays, his story about shooting one at the end of a spearfishing trip and putting it into the bottom of their boat, just an idle shot, he said, for no one ate stingrays, and how the ray sent its barb through one of the oar locks and my father kept that oarlock with the stingray barb on his desk. Never have I understood people's willingness to swim with stingrays — nor, for that matter, my father's carelessness.

We put on our hiking gear on the beach and walked through the mangroves past the dark orange crocodile ponds. Byron's son, Adam, was with us, and he ran ahead along the faint path that skirted the ponds. Was Byron not afraid the crocs would attack his son? I have heard Byron on radio and in front of many audiences saying our crocs are not aggressive, give them a healthy habitat and they are no threat to people. Talk about walking the talk, I thought, as I watched his son on the path beside the crocodile ponds. And then we started to climb and the paths disappeared, stones turned underfoot, and although it was January, it was sweltering.

At first, I looked around at the Hellshire forest — small trees, epic heat, treacherous ground. The canopy dappled the fierce sun into trembling gold circles on the ground, the fallen leaves held the colours of autumn, rare patches of red-brown dirt hid in the crevices of white limestone rock. Soon I was too out of breath to notice anything but where to find secure footing.

My vision darkened at the last steep stretch and I had to sit. I wet the small scarf around my neck from my water bottle and wiped my face, ashamed of being weak, mourning my younger self who could have run up the trail, as surefooted as Byron's son. Fred stayed with me while the others went ahead and in one of those wordless moments of marriage, I knew he was thinking: why are we here again? I wasn't sure myself. It is enough for me that the Hellshire forest exists, that Antarctic penguins raise their chicks in huddled colonies, that blue whales roam the deepest seas, even if I have never seen them. I got up and we climbed the last bit into the south camp, past a pile of bleached out pig skulls — the remains of some of the enemies of the Jamaican iguana.

The camp iguana, Stumpy, waited, eating iceberg lettuce. He had no tail and was perfectly camouflaged for Hellshire. Despite his pet status, he retained the dignity of age and harsh survivorship. I sat on a wooden platform and looked out over the unbroken forest canopy to the coast, another kind of trackless sea, its complexities hidden, poorly understood, insufficiently valued. I drank and tried to eat a bit of my sandwich. Eventually, Fred and I walked together along some of the trails, Byron explaining the trapping process, and we saw two more wild iguanas. They were not animals to make you catch your breath at their beauty or grace, but I was glad I saw them that day in the Hellshire forest.

When we went back to the boat, the members of the field team were waiting with a trussed up wild pig, black and bloody, found in one of the traps. It was returning with us in the boat to the mainland, where it would be butchered, killed, and eaten. Too much reality, I thought. It was fine to consider the killing of pigs, cats, and mongooses in the abstract for the Greater Good of the survival of the iguana, but the doomed pig was troubling. I didn't object, though. I told myself it was pointless. And it was: this was the world we had made, where to save one species, living animals had to be sacrificed. The pig was heaved into the boat and we smashed our way through those big waves past Wreck Reef, me holding on tightly, trying to take the pounding by flexing my knees, thinking about my fragile bones and the tortured pig and how difficult it is to undo humanity's reckless mistakes and the many known and unknown casualties of dominion.

And then, a few months after the Goat Islands rumours started, our current environment minister, the Hon. Robert Pickersgill, went to Beijing and from there came the announcement — yes, the Government of Jamaica was giving "very serious consideration" to the building of a large transshipment port on or near to the Goat Islands in the Portland Bight Protected Area. Details were few, but any port would result in dredging, excavation, land reclamation, and devastation of the marine environment. At the time, I was at a workshop for a new grant we had just received to carry out a research project on the government's progress under Jamaica's Access to Information Act. Coincidentally, one of the partners in this initiative was the Caribbean Coastal Area Management Foundation (CCAM), the NGO managing the Portland Bight Protected Area. The workshop proceedings were suspended and we called a press conference, and the press came, and I did take a moment to think back to the early days of JET when there would have been no way a group of senior journalists would have come to a hastily called press conference on an environmental issue. While we put together maps and images and a presentation, the Minister of Transport, the Hon. Omar Davies, called me on my cell phone to ask if there was any way, any way at all, that a port could coexist with "the environment."

You will annihilate it, Minister, I told him, and he rang off. Later, I saw him interviewed on TV and he objected to the use of words like "annihilate" as being "sensationalist," but his body language was embarrassed and I thought he probably knew it was the right word. Later, he disparaged the issue of whether or not to ignore the four laws and three international conventions protecting Portland Bight and the Goat Islands as being about "two likkle lizaad."

For the next eighteen months, the fight to save Goat Islands and the surrounding coast took up most of my time and energy. Along with what seemed to me to be far too few people, I went to meetings, organised trips to the islands, printed t-shirts, developed a website, made a calendar (and presented copies to a head table of government bigwigs at the launch of a recycling company), critiqued an environmental scoping report, wrote articles and letters to everyone imaginable, did Access to Information requests (most were denied), and finally, filed legal action to ask the court to review the denials of access.

The personal abuse arrived. A large headline in one of our daily newspapers invited me to go to hell. A columnist referred to his wet dreams about me. Another one suggested I was "screeching" without mentioning my name — which somehow annoyed me more than if he had made it incontestable who he was talking about. And every media article attracted scores of comments, many of which suggested "that woman" was going to ruin Jamaica's economic future. Then I started receiving phone calls suggesting I should be careful, for life was cheap in Jamaica. When there were three such calls in a twenty-four-hour period from people I had to take seriously, I acknowledged being afraid.

Not that it was the first time. To stand for nature is to stand against powerful and potentially ruthless economic forces. Could my job, my vocation, get me killed? I thought of my son and my husband, my two sisters, my friends — how could risking a bullet at my gate possibly be worth it?

Well, I told myself, you're just not that important. Not much of a threat to anyone. I spoke with a few politicians and Cabinet members about the phone calls, they made reassuring noises, and in time, the Goat Islands port disappeared from the headlines. Every now and then, I sent out a half-hearted letter asking about the status. Most were never answered.

And then on 22 September, 2016, I was idly checking my Twitter feed and I saw a Tweet from our new prime minister, the Hon. Andrew Holness, who was at a town hall meeting in New York: "In essence, despite some media reports, the government will not be allowing a port at Goat Islands." I read it over and over. Had any natural resource in the world ever been saved by a tweet? The prime minister was responding to a question put to him from the floor — Mr Prime Minister, what's happening about Goat Islands? Who was the person who asked that question and why? What had he or she read or seen? Had they ever seen the bulk of the islands against the rising sun? Were they or their families from Old Harbour Bay? It was enormous that someone had spoken for two small islands in the Caribbean Sea at a town hall meeting in New York.

Now, I work to see if the long-held plans to declare the island a sanctuary for the Jamaican iguana can be revived. Getting a simple acknowledgment of a letter takes six months and a meeting between government stakeholders has yet not been possible.

"No man is an island, entire of itself," wrote John Donne in 1623. Carl Safina, in his 2003 book *Eye of the Albatross*, wrote: "No island is an island." Dr Safina wrote those words after witnessing an albatross trying unsuccessfully to feed her chick because of a plastic toothbrush stuck in the adult bird's gullet. He was on Midway Atoll in the North Pacific at the time, surely one of the remotest islands in the world, half way between North America and Asia, almost three thousand nautical miles from San Francisco, over two thousand from Tokyo. Yet, despite its remoteness, the stamp of man is all over it, in its runways and remnants of warfare, and in the plastic that now litters its shores.

Midway is a coral atoll almost five miles across, with three small islands, located in the Northwestern Hawaiian Islands, now the Papahanaumokuakea Marine National Monument — one of the largest marine protected areas in the world. More than seven thousand species are found in the Monument, a quarter of which are found nowhere else in the world, and the islands are used by over three million seabirds for resting, nesting, and foraging. Midway is at the northern limit of coral growth in the Pacific, and its reefs shelter about two hundred marine species. Our human constructs of borders in the sea, our good intentions announced in workshops at the United Nations, cannot stop waste at those borders. The vast waters of the Pacific have become a soup of plastic. It is now nearly four hundred years since John Donne used the word "island" as a metaphor for a place of impenetrable isolation, and in that time we have made a world where there is nowhere — literally nowhere — that remains entire of itself.

Jamaica: island of islands. The smaller islands are microcosms of the largest one, and here are the central facts. We are surrounded by the sea. Every plant, animal, and human has come here from somewhere else. We are a mountain that is an island and our mythology is Biblical. In Deleuze's words: . . . the ark sets down on the one place on earth that remains uncovered by water, a circular and sacred place, from which the world begins anew. It is an island or a mountain, or both at once; the island is a mountain under water, and the mountain, an island that is still dry. Here we see creation caught in a re-creation, which is concentrated in a holy land in the middle in the ocean. The island, according to Deleuze, is a cosmic egg, entrusted to man and not the gods. So far, we have not been worthy stewards.

THE WAYWARD SON

Vashti Bowlah

As she held up the thread for the third time, she heard the sound of crackling tyres. It wasn't that long ago when she could easily find the eye of a needle. She suddenly felt two decades older than her forty-seven years. She glided her spectacles down the ridge of her nose with her right index finger, the torn white shirt resting on her lap. A police car had pulled up on the gravel path next to the flower bed, almost crushing the scarf of marigolds covering the ground. The lone uniformed officer exited the vehicle. She recognised Constable Dave Ramsey. She rose from her rocker and placed the shirt over the armrest after pinning the needle through the fabric to secure it. She leaned over the front porch, her heart racing. Her hands tightened around the wooden banister when he asked for her son.

She returned minutes later with Rudy close behind. He signalled for the boy to move closer as they descended the three steps leading to the front yard.

When asked about a break in at Corporal Jit's house, Rudy looked up to the sky with squinted eyes, "Thursday?"

"Yeah, day before yesterday," he clarified. "Where you was that evening?"

"I was in school 'til half past two, and then I take a taxi to come home. But when I drop off, I went in the shop first to buy a notebook."

"Which shop? The one next to the corporal house?"

"Well . . . yeah . . . is right next door." He lifted his shoulders up and down. "I always go there because it near the junction and on the way home."

Constable Ramsey subjected him to close scrutiny. "How much years you have now, about fourteen?"

"I go be fifteen next month."

"Well, I know you since you born and I don't want you to get in no trouble, so you sure you know nothing about a break in? Because if you lying . . ."

"I not lying."

She could think of nothing to say in support of her son, because she wasn't sure of his actions lately. Constable Ramsey expressed his concern about something he heard at the station and was looking into it. He assured her there was nothing to worry about once Rudy was telling the truth. He returned to the vehicle and sped off.

Silence hung between them. Was it Thursday he had skipped class, or Wednesday? Did he skip class so he could break into Jit's house? But why? And why didn't Jit mention anything? No . . . no, she needed to believe her son.

She knew every bad word that was whispered about him, some of which she overheard with her own ears while at the shop, by the seamstress, or the market vendor. The complaints all began when he started hanging out with Lenny over a year ago. Sometimes, it was the villager who saw them picking his coconuts; another who swore they stole her two ducks; or the farmer who claimed they broke into his tool shed. During investigations, none were able to say for sure that they had actually seen them do it, only that it could have been one or the other. Most of these reports were brought to her attention by her neighbour and dear friend. Molly was good at heart and much like the older sister she never had, but they didn't call her Radio 610 for nothing. At times, it would seem as though she heard the news before it happened. Just then, the familiar voice penetrated her thoughts.

"Hai Bhagwan."

Chanmatie lifted her hands above her head. "Speak of the devil."

"What is that you say?" asked Molly.

"Um . . . the yard over here . . . I was telling Rudy it not level," was her quick reply.

Molly tried to catch her breath. "I just now see Dave here and I want him to do something for me, but he drive off so fast while I was crossing the road. Now I go have to wait 'til he come home later." Her eyes darted from mother to son. "But anyways, what he was doing here? Something wrong?"

Jit interrupted the scene when he rode into the yard on his bicycle, his preferred mode of transport that once belonged to his grandfather. He secured it against the front teak post. "What Ramsey was doing here?"

"I was just asking she the same thing," Molly threw in.

Chanmatie ignored her neighbour, who was anxiously awaiting her reply. "I go talk to you later, I going and cook now." Molly plastered an agreeable expression on her round face, stating that she also had to cook before her husband returned. She crossed the narrow dirt road to her house, twice looking over her shoulder before disappearing through her front door.

Jit repeated his question in a commanding voice. Rudy stepped in front of the corporal, throwing him a glacial stare, then a warning glance at his mother before storming into the house. With concern in her eyes, she watched until he was out of earshot.

"How come you never say nothing about a break in by you?" she demanded of Jit.

She hoped for a satisfactory explanation, but none came. Instead, he grew tense, stating it was nobody's business. Moments later, he pulled her closer, circling her waist as he tried to steal a kiss. She turned and it landed on her cheek. The scent of alcohol on his breath disturbed her. He was visibly upset when she refused his advances.

"You done work or you now going?" She switched the topic.

"I just finish three o'clock and the first thing I do is come to see you, but you always have some excuse why I can't touch you." He attempted to kiss her again. She gave him a gentle push and escaped to the house.

The music from Rudy's room was turned up louder than before. It was his usual Saturday routine — wake up around midday, then listen to music on his transistor radio all afternoon. He would not emerge again until Jit had left. Rudy had made no attempt to get along with him since Jit and Chanmatie started a relationship over three months ago. They barely said two words to each other on the rare occasion when they crossed paths.

How could she explain to Rudy that she could never forget his father, or that she was not trying to replace him. His death had been sudden and the driver was never found after he fled the scene of the accident, leaving him bleeding and alone along the side of the dirt road. The last two years had been devastating as she tried to piece her life back together. The elders in the village were right — it was only the good ones who were taken away too soon, because her Ramesh had been a good man.

Though he was nothing like her late husband, she had known Jit since childhood. They grew up in the same village, attended the same schools and played together as children. She was saddened when his wife had succumbed to injuries she received from a fall three years ago, so she knew he also felt the pain of losing a loved one. He had been supportive during her husband's funeral, even offering to help with the expenses. He turned up at regular intervals while she continued to mourn, especially at times when she needed someone to talk to. She would have been an ungrateful woman had she turned him away.

Jit entered the back door while she sat cutting up a bundle of bodi. He lounged back next to her on the lone sofa, taking a sip of alcohol from the flask he carried. She shook her head and turned up her nose. He stretched his arm across her shoulders, allowing his fingers to linger where they should not have. They had argued several times before about his drinking, so she decided to make this his last visit.

Rudy strolled into the kitchen just after noon the next day, brushing his fingers back through his thick mass of hair . . . so much like his father. He sucked his teeth when he saw the contents in the small iron pot sitting on the stove.

"I know you don't like cassava, but Jit bring some the other day so I have to use it. Look, I grating some now to bake a pone."

"Well, I don't want nothing from he," protested Rudy, sitting across from her at the old wooden table.

She pointed to the covered plate on the counter. "I make some rice for you to eat with the chicken, I will get it for you."

She set the plate down in front of him with a glass of homemade mauby. Her heart softened a little. "I know Jit a long time and thought it woulda be good to have somebody around who is a police so we go feel safe."

"So when he hit you the other day, you did feel safe that time? Or you feel I didn't know?" He watched as she continued grating the cassava on the grater he and his father had made from an empty Klim tin for an end-of-term art and craft project. Suddenly he sprang to his feet, moving closer with one long stride before she even realised it. "What is that by your eye? Don't tell me he hit you again? He hit you, Ma? You let him hit you again!" He pounded his fist on the table in a helpless gesture. "I feel you does get stupid when he around, because the mother I know woulda never take that from nobody!"

"Was a lil argument we had, and I handle it already."

"Let me guess," he responded angrily. "You ask him 'bout what Constable Dave say and he get vex and mistake you for a punching bag. And from the way he was looking, I wouldn't be surprise if he was drunk too."

He wasn't completely accurate, she thought, but his version was easier to accept.

He shook his head, on the verge of tears. "Pa had more breeding in he little toe than that fool go ever have, but one of these days you go see he true colours."

"You not so perfect, you know, because since you liming with that Lenny, I always getting a complain. I does feel I can't handle you no more." She was already sorry by the time the words escaped her lips, but the damage was already done.

He wiped at the tears meandering from his eyes. "Well, I real sorry for disappointing you just because I grow up," he said, moving towards his bedroom door, leaving his food and drink untouched.

There was nothing more she could say. He was already upset she had made him cut the grass and pull out the weeds in the flowerbeds as punishment for skipping school last week. At least the principal took pity on a poor mother after she had begged him not to suspend her son. It was good to keep him busy. He had even turned Lenny away when he came to meet him recently, including last Friday while he was cleaning the flowerbeds. She prayed for her son, holding on to that glimmer of hope.

After school on Monday, Rudy hid inside the shop next to Jit's house. It wasn't long before he saw the hulking figure arrive on his bicycle. He darted across and watched from behind the hibiscus fence in his front yard. By the time Jit unlocked his front door, Rudy had snuck up behind him, both standing on the inside of the doorway. Jit's surprise was evident.

Rudy waved a finger in Jit's face. "You better don't hit my mother again!"

Jit grabbed the boy's wrist with a sinister smile. "What wrong with you, boy? I could lock you up anytime I want."

"And you could get lock up too for beating up a woman, you drunk coward!" Rudy retorted, trying to wriggle out of his hold.

"Look here, little boy, that is between me and she." He grabbed hold of Rudy's other hand as he flung it towards him.

"Well, you better watch your back if you even think about hitting she again."

"You lucky I like your mother, otherwise I take you down to the station right now."

"Lucky me! Is a good thing you didn't hate she!" Rudy connected his knee to his groin.

Jit folded over, grimacing in pain, but not before shoving Rudy out the door so hard that he almost fell. Rudy struggled to maintain his balance and walked up to him again, staring him in his eyes. "By the way Corporal, the next time you too drunk to remember where you leave your gun, don't say that somebody break into your house and take it."

Rudy was contented for the moment with the shock and confusion reflected in Jit's eyes. Jit was too drunk that evening when he placed his gun on their bureau and didn't even realise it. All Rudy had to do was sneak it into his room before his mother saw it. One side of his mouth curled upwards as he calmly walked away.

Rudy dragged his feet through the living room and threw his green canvas bag on his bed. He lingered near the doorway to his mother's bedroom after catching a glimpse of her sprawled on her back, her right arm swung over her face to block off the light. She too hadn't eaten the previous evening. She looked so peaceful. Such a contrast to not so long ago, when the entire village knew when she was angry about one thing or the other. Her small frame was never a true representation of her thunderous voice and temperament.

Sensing his presence, she rose and sat on the edge of the bed pressing her fingers to her temples. "I didn't realise it was so late. I lie down a little bit and sleep away in the breeze. I didn't even cook nothing yet."

He offered to eat the slice of pone she had left for him the day before. He thought of all the hard work she had put into making the pone, only because she knew he liked it. When she asked about his day at school, he reflected on when his teacher made him stand in a corner in front of the class because he didn't do his homework. He never liked maths or algebra. He was certain he would never have to use any of those formulas in his lifetime, so what was the need to learn them. He also reflected on his confrontation with Jit.

"School was okay, Ma," he lied. "But I have plenty homework to do."

Darkness descended without warning, the narrow dirt roads of Sugarcane Valley deserted by the time he was halfway through his homework. The rain had been threatening throughout the day, dark clouds still circling above, a cool wind whistling through the trees. Rudy sprinted to the front window upon hearing the loud crack on their galvanised roof, just in time to see the silhouette of two boys running off in the direction of a winding dirt track. He knew exactly who they were.

His mother stepped out from the kitchen into the small living room, a dishcloth in one hand and enamel plate in the other. She also had heard the noise and was not convinced when he shrugged it off.

"But that sound like if something fall on the roof." Her head swivelled from left to right.

"The wind must be blow down a dry branch from the mango tree." He closed the curtains and returned to his book.

"Hai Bhagwan! I sure is them troublesome boys and them up

to some mischief." She pulled the curtains and looked out the other window, her eyes searching in all directions until she was satisfied there was no one. "Try to finish your homework early in case the lights cut off in this kinda weather." She returned to the kitchen mumbling something about those good-for-nothing children who don't listen to their parents.

Rudy breathed a sigh of relief. Jit thought he could scare him by sending his nephew and Lenny to pelt stones on their roof as a warning, but he didn't scare easily. He focused on the remaining questions, reading them over and over again, but the numbers only danced around in the pages. He was sure they were laughing at him too while they did their victory dance. He thought he understood the formula in class but it made no sense to him now. He eventually retired to his room.

Molly came calling bright and early the next morning carrying two transparent plastic bags. Chanmatie greeted her at the entrance to the front porch and accepted the bag of tomatoes and a generous slice of pumpkin. She expressed her appreciation. Molly remained on the front step, her eyes darting in and out of the house.

"Come inside if you want, I shelling some peas while they fresh."

She looked around, "Rudy gone to school already?"

"Not yet, you want to see him?"

"No-no, I want to tell you something but I don't want him to hear."

Chanmatie wore a look of concern, throwing her hands in the air. "Hai Bhagwan. Just say what you have to say for God's sake, you making me nervous."

"Okay-okay, but I don't know how you going take this." Molly leaned forward, lowering her voice while her eyes remained fixed on the front doorway. "Anyways, I hear it was Jit who knock down Ramesh on the road. He did finish he shift and was going back to the station when it happen. I hear he use a police car that day to go down by Ramlal Bar and he was real drunk, so he didn't want nobody to find out because he coulda lose he job."

Chanmatie felt as if the floor had opened up under her feet, leaving her weightless and adrift. She was suffocating from the growing lump in her throat, feeling as if she might faint. "You . . . you don't know what you saying, Molly. I . . . I does always listen to everything you say, but you can't expect me to believe that."

"I wouldn't tell you if I wasn't sure, but it bothering me since I find out last night. Dave didn't want to say nothing but I harass him until he tell me. He say he investigating a week now since he hear Jit talking to a next officer. It reach the senior officers now so I don't know what go happen to him." Molly clasped her hands around hers. "I had to tell you because you like a sister to me, and you know Dave does always look out for you and Rudy, since . . ."

Both women were startled by the creaking of the wooden floor, unaware of how long Rudy had been standing in the doorway. He wore his white shirt with monogrammed pocket and long black pants, his green canvas bag slung across his left shoulder. He glanced at Molly before locking eyes with his mother, his face void of emotion. He acknowledged them and left.

Chanmatie could not focus on anything else after Molly's revelation. She washed the clothes with too much bleach, added too much curry and less salt to the peas, and sliced her finger with the kitchen knife. She had known Jit almost her entire life, but did she really know him? If he lied about a break-in at his home, what else could he lie about? And . . . she never thought he would hit her . . . or try to force himself on her in a drunken state . . . yet he did. Did his late wife really slip and fall so many times over the years? No one could be that clumsy.

She decided she would use the afternoon to complete some errands. Molly had given her a lot to digest and it was best to clear her mind or risk going insane. She suspected that Jit would return to try and make amends, and she needed to be mentally prepared. She picked up a few sewing supplies at the haberdashery store, paid the electricity bill, and bought a new school shirt and merino for Rudy.

Chanmatie was relieved when Dave pulled up at the taxi stand in his Datsun pickup. He was on his way home after running some errands and did not hesitate to stop. She had just left the vegetable market and was grateful that she would not have to carry her heavy bags. She couldn't thank him enough after he dropped her off at her front yard, politely refusing his offer to take her bags into the house. When he hesitated to leave, she followed his eyes to Jit's bicycle which was secured against the front teak post. He insisted on checking in on them when he was leaving in a few minutes to take up his shift.

She heard the commotion just as she entered the front door. She dropped her bags against the front wall and followed the muffled sounds coming from behind the sofa. She was shocked to see Jit punching Rudy repeatedly while he pinned him to the floor. Blood was streaming down her son's face and she grew frantic. She grabbed the back of Jit's collar and tried with all her might to lift him off without success. She then started pounding his back with both fists, all the while screaming for him to stop. Jit spun around, startled by the sight of her. Rudy seized the moment and pushed him off, scrambling to his feet and into his room.

"What the hell!" she exploded. "You were hitting my son! You . . . you sick bastard . . . you were hitting my son!"

"That wayward son of yours started it," he replied, "accusing me of all kinda things."

"Like knocking down his father and leaving him for dead on the side of the road?" she raged, as the floor seemed to rock under her.

He froze, jaw dropped, eyes wide open.

"Yeah, I know everything," she nodded, "so just get out of my house before I do something I won't regret!"

"The two of you gone mad!" was his only response before turning to leave.

"Corporal!" Rudy got both their attentions. He was holding a gun which Jit was all too familiar with, his bloody face a mask of hate and anger. Chanmatie could sense the tremors within his slim frame as he took aim at his target. Jit remained still. She too stood there . . . too shocked to do anything else. There was no time to think, or talk him out of it. Rudy's finger was already on the trigger. She threw herself against Jit so they both tumbled to the floor. The bullet went through the front window, shattering the frosted glass louvre, the loud bang ringing in her ears.

She sprang up within seconds, making a mad dash towards her son who was poised to take another shot. She stopped in front of him and silently prayed, reciting every prayer she could remember. Her heart was thudding fast and loud and she swallowed to relieve the dryness in her throat. She reached for his hand that held the gun, releasing her breath when his arms eventually dropped to his sides. She wrapped her arms around him and buried his face against her bosom. She thought she heard the sound of crackling tyres, then footsteps. Molly was standing in the doorway, her hands covering her mouth. Dave was close behind, now dressed in his full police uniform. Jit was still on the floor, sweating profusely.

"What you gone and do that for, Ma? It was he! That rotten, stinkin' drunk knock down my pa and leave him for dead." The tears were flowing freely down his cheeks, his school uniform stained with blood and tears. His chin quivered and his lips fell apart. "And . . . and he hit you, Ma. He hit you. Pa never hit you."

"I not as stupid as you think you know, son. I tell him already that I don't want him here no more." Her voice was tender, her heart aching for the terrible pain he felt. "I know now what kinda man he is."

"Then, why, Ma, why you didn't let him die? Why you save him for?"

She thought of what would have happened to her only child had he shot Jit. His life, his education, his entire future would have been ruined because of one bad deed; one that any mother would forgive. Still consoling him against her bosom like the child he was, she replied, "I wasn't trying to save him son, I was saving you."

THREE POEMS

Shivanee Ramlochan

THE YOUNG INDIAN WITCH LEARNS HOW TO PRAY

When my mother asks, what made you
I spin the prayer mat of our family tree to face her, tell her
pick a man:
- my uncle, the alcoholic
- my uncle, the welder of nursery pornographies
- my uncle, the vicious flirt
- my uncle, the disappearer of alms
- my uncle, the golden tooth in the kindergarten night.
Where else did I learn my deceit but at Sunday puja?

I sat under the glass eye
of the lecher-pundit, one hand spanning his conch,
the other under his white dhoti, praying in half-jerks.
The yellow nail of his littlest finger curled, catching ghee and
    sweat.

When he blew, I felt the echoes of God under my palms, a lesson
that the Lord can disturb you anywhere without consent.
When the pundit swept me into a kiss, I smelled farm milk
and cow shit, wet grass and pig feed. I turned my face.
The pundit bundled me into the arms of all my uncles.
He promised one day he would get his kiss.

Now,
I uproot unwanted men like loose jhandis,
kicking them out of the red earth that baked them, discarding
their thoraxes in shattered lutes of clay.

THE NAMELESS GIRL AND THE NATURES OF BLOOD

The girl buries her first bleeding in the epicentre of the island.

Five days after, the island offers her killing weed,

curled like a plait of bread in her shrine for small godfolk.

Motherless, fatherless, she sucks and spits it into a brew.

She uses cave water, storm warning, shelter roots to stir it.

The girl does not know she is a girl, but she knows that she bleeds.

Each moon rinses her bare,

pulls red from her like an ibis witch, dissolving homes.

She rinses the tentacles of her second bleeding in the deep ocean,
    feels

the spray rush for it, greedier than the sun on her cut lip.

After the night of her third bleeding,

every bird she touches sings the hymn of its own funeral,

turning tufted throats upwards as their eyes glass

in time to their final notes.

With each moon, the island surrenders a murder for her blood.

She learns to watch for the deaths, skins and cures them, covers

them in salt and ganja, learns to brew them in places

too holy for names. She learns to be careful with what she holds.

One morning, she wakes to find the waters red at her feet.

On the horizon, a boat perches, stout and waiting.

The girl who does not know she is a girl feels her heart pummel
    itself raw, manchineel-ready. She
reaches, slow, into caves where she has nursed her poisons and
    griefs,
drags them out by scruff and thorn-nape, sets them to the shore.

She rises, pregnant with six months of murders,
and scales the limestone promontory facing the sea.
She does not know what a boat is,
but bleeding has taught her to understand invasions.
The boat encroaches and she arches, moon-dappled in a bleeding,
eager to unleash her deaths.

My Father and His Father Before Him

Growing up, you learned

how to flutter the blades of your shoulders

fast as hummingbirds drunk on sugar

to keep a cutlass from kissing your spine.

Growing up, you were always

running from something sharp,

missiling through cane high like your waist.

You learned everything is a wingspan away from war:

a card game,

a cooking night,

a capsised curry bowl leaking into the grout.

You didn't blame your father. There are

no pictures for what your aja did to him.

There is no way your father could have moved that fast.

When my aja died, you went to his room,

unhooked the harmonium he never let you hold in life.

Your hands knew the ragas without being taught.

The blades of your shoulders moved like hummingbirds,

hovering in prayer.

Alone in your father's music, you vibrated,

swallowing all the small wars between you like tears.

AFTERWORD

There are moments in time when the elements are in tune, the stars line up, and extraordinary things happen. The birth of the Hollick Arvon Prize was such a moment.

The partnership between the Hollick Family Charitable Trust, The Bocas Lit Fest, Arvon, and the Rogers, Coleridge and White literary agency emerged from old friendships between people committed to the creative industries and to literature in particular. Sue Woodford-Hollick and Marina Salandy-Brown, both with Caribbean roots, understood the need of the region to start reclaiming the glory days of West Indian writing and to harness the talent that exists up and down the Caribbean's thousand miles of island shores, but which is frustrated by the distance between the beautiful archipelago and the literary metropolis. Ruth Borthwick of Arvon and Deborah Rogers, the now deceased co-founder of one of London's premier literary agencies, spent their professional lives outing and growing some of the world's best writers.

We came together to create this prize that has provided a

unique opportunity for many emerging writers, especially women writers, to present their work to larger audiences, and which has also enabled the winners to be mentored, tutored, promoted, agented, and published. The three winners have now all published books and gone on to win other prizes.

Our organisations have all witnessed the unpredictable climate in the world of books as tastes change, funding ebbs and flows, and technology transforms our world, but the human need to express our deepest emotions and thoughts never subsides. The endless seeking to make sense of all aspects of life and the human condition is constant, and it feels important to be part of that constancy.

We wish all the writers whose excellent work appears in this anthology much success in their literary lives. And we urge them to keep writing, as we need to hear their voices.

Marina Salandy-Brown
Bocas Lit Fest

Sue Woodford-Hollick
Hollick Family
Charitable Trust

Ruth Borthwick
Arvon

Jennifer Hewson
Rogers, Coleridge and White

ABOUT THE EDITOR

Funso Aiyejina is a poet, short story writer, and playwright, born in Nigeria and living in Trinidad and Tobago. He is Professor Emeritus and former Dean of the Faculty of Humanities and Education at the University of the West Indies, St Augustine. His collection of short fiction, *The Legend of the Rockhills and Other Stories*, won the 2000 Commonwealth Writers' Prize for Best First Book (Africa). He is a widely published critic on African and West Indian literature and culture, and deputy director of the NGC Bocas Lit Fest, Trinidad and Tobago's annual literary festival. He is the author of *Earl Lovelace* (Caribbean Biography Series).

ABOUT THE CONTRIBUTORS

Lisa Allen-Agostini is a writer and editor from Trinidad and Tobago. She is the author of the young adult novel *Home Home* (forthcoming from Papillote Press in 2018), the tween action-adventure novel *The Chalice Project* (Macmillan Caribbean), and the collection of poems *Swallowing the Sky* (Cane Arrow Press). She co-edited the anthology *Trinidad Noir* (Akashic Books).

Nicolette Bethel was born and raised in Nassau, the Bahamas, where she currently resides. She has lived, studied, and worked in the UK and Canada, and served as Director of Culture for the Bahamas for five years. She is currently Assistant Professor of Sociology at the College of the Bahamas, and serves as Head of the Department of

Psychology, Sociology, and Social Work. She is the founder of the Shakespeare in Paradise theatre festival (est. 2009) and of Ringplay Productions theatre company (est. 2001). She is a playwright, poet, fiction writer, and anthropologist.

Danielle Boodoo-Fortuné is a Trinidadian poet and artist. Her writing and art have appeared in publications such as *Bim: Arts for the 21st Century, The Caribbean Writer, Small Axe Literary Salon, Anthurium: A Caribbean Studies Journal.* She is the winner of the 2018 *Wasafiri* New Writing Prize, the 2015 Hollick Arvon Caribbean Writers Prize, and the 2013 Montreal Poetry Prize, among other awards. Her debut book, *Doe Songs*, is published by Peepal Tree Press in 2018.

Vashti Bowlah is a writer from Trinidad and Tobago, author of *Under the Peepal Tree.* Her stories have also appeared in international publications such as *The Caribbean Writer, St Petersburg Review, Poui, WomanSpeak Journal,* and Akashic's Duppy Thursday series, among others. She also has a short story forthcoming in the anthology *Sunspot Jungle: The Ever Expanding Universe of SFF.* Her fiction centres on the humble lifestyle, culture, and traditions of East Indians in Trinidad and Tobago.

Richard Georges is the author of *Make Us All Islands* (Shearsman Books) and *Giant* (Platypus Press). His poems have appeared or are forthcoming in *Prelude, Smartish Pace, The Puritan, wildness, The Poetry Review, Wasafiri,* and elsewhere. In 2017, he was shortlisted for the Forward Prize's Felix Dennis Prize for Best First Collection. He lives and works in the British Virgin Islands.

Zahra Gordon is a Trinidad-based poet who has been published in literary journals such as *Amistad, Mantis, phat'itude, Kalyani, TRAUE,* and *The New Engagement.* She is a Callaloo Creative Writing

Workshop and CaribLit Residential Writing Programme fellow, and winner of the 2010 Furious Flower Poetry Competition. Gordon is an alumna of Howard University.

Barbara Jenkins was born in Trinidad. Since she started writing in 2008, her stories have won the Commonwealth Short Story Prize, Caribbean Region, in 2010 and 2011; the *Wasafiri* New Writing Prize; the Canute Brodhurst Prize for short fiction, awarded by *The Caribbean Writer;* the *Small Axe* Short Story Competition; and other awards. In 2013 she was named winner of the inaugural Hollick Arvon Caribbean Writers Prize. Her debut short story collection, *Sic Transit Wagon* (Peepal Tree Press, 2013) was awarded the Guyana Prize for Literature Caribbean Award, and her novel *De Rightest Place* is published in 2018.

Lelawattee Manoo-Rahming is a Trinidadian-Bahamian mechanical/building services engineer, poet, fiction writer, artist, and essayist. She is the author of two poetry collections, *Curry Flavour* (Peepal Tree Press, 2000) and *Immortelle and Bhandaaraa Poems* (Proverse Hong Kong, 2011). Currently she is working on her first collection of short stories and her third collection of poems. Her work has also appeared in numerous publications including *WomanSpeak, The Caribbean Writer, Poui,* and *Interviewing the Caribbean,* as well as the online journals *Zocalo Poets, The Muse,* the Commonwealth Foundation's *addastories,* and Akashic's Duppy Thursday series.

Sharon Millar was born and lives in Trinidad. She is the co-winner of the 2013 Commonwealth Short Story Prize and the 2012 Small Axe Literary Competition for fiction. Her first collection, *The Whale House and Other Stories* (Peepal Tree Press, 2015), was longlisted for the 2016 OCM Bocas Prize and her work has been anthologised in *Pepperpot: Best New Stories from the Caribbean* (Peekash Press,

2014) and *Trinidad Noir 2: The Classics* (Akashic Books, 2016). She is currently at work on her first novel.

Ira Mathur is an India-born multimedia journalist living in Trinidad and Tobago. She has been working as a journalist and columnist for the past twenty years, winning eleven local and regional awards for excellence. In 2015 Mathur was chosen by the UK literary agent Clare Alexander of Aitken Alexander Associates to submit her work. Her piece in *Thicker Than Water* is an excerpt from a book-length work in progress. Find out more at iramathur.org.

Diana McCaulay is an award-winning Jamaican writer and environmental activist. She has written four novels, *Dog-Heart* (2010), *Huracan* (2012), *Gone to Drift* (2016), and *White Liver Gal* (2017). She was the Caribbean regional winner of the Commonwealth Short Story Prize in 2012, for her short story "The Dolphin Catchers". Her fiction has also appeared in *Eleven Eleven, Granta* online, *Fleeting Magazine, The Caribbean Writer,* and the Jamaica Observer's literary supplement, *Bookends,* among other publications.

Monica Minott is a chartered accountant and poet, author of the book *Kumina Queen.* She has received two awards in the Jamaican National Book Development Council's annual literary competitions for book-length collections of her poetry. She was awarded first prize in the inaugural *Small Axe* Literary Competition for poetry. Her poems have been published in *The Caribbean Writer, Small Axe, Cultural Voice Magazine, SX Salon, BIM,* and the anthologies *Jubilation* and *Coming Up Hot.*

Philip Nanton is an Honorary Research Associate at University of Birmingham, UK. He lectures occasionally at the University of the West Indies, Cave Hill, Barbados. His recent publications include

Island Voices from St Christopher and the Barracudas (2014), *Canouan Suite and Other Pieces* (2016), both from Papillote Press, and *Frontiers of the Caribbean* (2017), from Manchester University Press.

Xavier Navarro Aquino was born and raised in Puerto Rico. His fiction is forthcoming in *McSweeney's Quarterly Concern* and has appeared in *Guernica*, *The Literary Review*, and *Day One*. He has published poetry in *The Caribbean Writer*. He was a work-study scholar at the Bread Loaf Writers' Conference in 2014 and received a travel scholarship to Ghana, Spain, and Morocco in 2014 from the University of Puerto Rico, Río Piedras where he earned an MA in English Caribbean Studies. He is currently a PhD candidate in English at the University of Nebraska-Lincoln.

Shivanee Ramlochan is a Trinidadian writer and book blogger. She is the Book Reviews Editor for *Caribbean Beat*. She writes about books for the NGC Bocas Lit Fest, the Caribbean's largest anglophone literary festival, and for Paper Based Books, Trinidad's oldest independent bookseller of Caribbean literature. She is the deputy editor of *The Caribbean Review of Books*. Her first book, *Everyone Knows I Am a Haunting*, was published by Peepal Tree Press in 2017.

Writer and editor **Judy Raymond** is based in Trinidad and was educated at the universities of Oxford and London. Her books include two biographical studies of contemporary Trinidadian artists, the goldsmith Barbara Jardine and fashion designer Meiling. *The Colour of Shadows: Images of Caribbean Slavery* (2016), was inspired by the work of the artist Richard Bridgens, who owned an estate in Trinidad in the closing years of Caribbean slavery. Her fourth book, to be published in 2018, is a short biography of Beryl McBurnie, who revived folk dance in Trinidad and founded the Little Carib Theatre.

Hazel Simmons-McDonald is Professor Emerita of Applied Linguistics and was the Pro-Vice Chancellor and Principal of the University of the West Indies Open Campus. She has edited anthologies of poetry and prose, and serves on the editorial board of *Poui*, a journal of creative writing. She has published poetry and short fiction.

Lynn Sweeting is a Bahamian writer who was a newspaper reporter writing on arts and culture in the 1980s before turning to writing poetry. Her poetry has been published in *The Caribbean Writer, Poui, Tongues of the Ocean, Small Axe,* and *Moko,* and anthologised in *Sisters of Caliban, A Multilingual Anthology of Writing by Women of the Caribbean,* and the Carifesta X anthology. Her prizes include *The Caribbean Writer's* Charlotte and Isidore Paiewonsky Prize for Poetry, a 1998 Pushcart nomination for her poem "Living on the Lee," and the 2014 Small Axe Literary Competition Second Prize for Poetry. She is founding editor and publisher of *WomanSpeak, A Journal of Writing and Art by Caribbean Women.*

Peta-Gaye V. Williams is a poet who was born and raised in Jamaica. Her awards include a JCDC bronze medal for Creative Writing Poetry (2013). She was the UWI Mona Poetry Clash champion in 2014 and 2015 and in 2016 she served as a judge for the competition. In 2014 she was the recipient of the Mervyn Morris Prize for Creative Writing Poetry, and in 2017 she received the John Reinecke Memorial Prize for the UWI Mona graduating student with the most outstanding academic performance in linguistics. She is currently working on her first collection of poetry.

ABOUT THE COVER ARTIST

Sandra Brewster is a Canadian artist based in Toronto. Her work has been exhibited nationally and abroad and explores themes of identity, representation and memory. Recent exhibitions in Toronto include *Common Cause: before and beyond the global,* Mercer Union; *Movers and Shakers,* Prefix Gallery; and *Here We Are Here,* Royal Ontario Museum. Additional exhibitions include *UnFixed Homelands,* Aljira Contemporary Art Centre, New Jersey; *New Found Lands,* Eastern Edge Gallery, St. John's, Newfoundland; and *Performing Blackness :: Performing Whiteness,* Allegheny Art Galleries, Meadville, Pennsylvania. Brewster's most recent solo exhibition, *It's All a Blur . . . ,* received the Gattuso Prize for outstanding featured exhibition at the CONTACT Photography Festival 2017. Brewster holds a Masters of Visual Studies from University of Toronto. She is represented by Georgia Scherman Projects.

Peekash Press is dedicated to publishing the work of emerging Caribbean writers living at home in the region, and presenting a new generation of literary talent to an international audience.

Begun in 2014 as a partnership between Peepal Tree Press in the United Kingdom and Akashic Books in the United States (hence the name), Peekash evolved from the CaribLit initiative, devised by the Bocas Lit Fest in partnership with Commonwealth Writers and the British Council.

In 2017, in keeping with the original intention to bring Peekash "home" to a physical base in the Caribbean, the Bocas Lit Fest assumed responsibility for the imprint.

Based in Port of Spain, Trinidad and Tobago, the Bocas Lit Fest is a not-for-profit organisation working to develop and promote Caribbean writers and writing, through an annual literary festival, a series of prizes, and year-round programmes and projects aimed at writer and reader development.

Visit www.bocaslitfest.com for more information.

9 781636 140216